Prologue

1943

Walter Simpkins waited until all the others were asleep, then he crept silently outside into the cool night air. He slipped into the shadows away from the barracks, far from any prying eyes. He could feel the pistol cold and hard in his hand. He had tears in his eyes and he swallowed hard. He had thought of leaving a note for his mum but he could not find the words. Besides, he had been so afraid Private Miller would find it. He could picture him, sniggering and jeering over his words and it was too hard to bear. Walter had tried. He had really tried to be a good soldier. He had joined up to do his duty and serve his country. His mum had been so proud of him. He was just eighteen. She had tearfully waved him off, telling him that his dad would have been proud too, if he had only lived to see the day. She had not wanted him to join up saying he was too young but she had seen the fierce determination in Walter's eyes and had reluctantly given her consent.

Walter had been afraid of fighting of course, but had not realised that there would be other things to be afraid of. It had all started innocently enough, Tommy Miller had seen the photo of his mother that Walter carried with him, and called him a mummy's boy. Then his friend Frank Gloucester had joined in with the ribbing. The rest of the men had photographs of their sweet hearts in their wallets. Walter had taken it in good part at first. He had expected a bit of leg pulling. That was part of being in the army. He had tried to give as good as he got, but Tommy Miller had turned nasty very quickly. He could dish it out but he could not take it, Walter thought sadly. He had called Walter a coward and a little poofter because he overheard him say that he was afraid of going into the front line once their basic training had finished. They were all afraid, despite their bravado. They would have been insane not to be afraid. Walter had been the only one brave enough to voice his fears. Tommy Miller had rewarded Walter's honesty by making his life a misery.

Walter could not take it anymore. Tommy and Frank had told Walter that he had better watch his back. When they reached the front line, they told him nastily, it was not the Germans he had to worry about; it was the two of them. Then they had laughed, flicked their cigarette butts at him and pushed him onto the dusty parade ground yet again.

They had constantly put dirt on his boots before inspection after he had spent hours polishing them. His immaculate bed had been messed up on a daily basis. His locker all but destroyed. They had drawn a beard and moustache on his precious irreplaceable photograph of his mother and pinned it up for everyone to laugh at. Tommy had even pissed on his freshly made bed last week, just before lights out. The Sarge had of course marched in and found him stripping the bed and had called him a filthy bed wetting little Nancy boy, and had ordered him to stand outside, holding the stinking wet sheets until the sun rose. The whole barracks had snickered together when the sergeant shouted at him. He had had to march round the parade ground carrying the pissy sheets as punishment for hours in the pouring rain. That had been bad enough, but facing the lads once he got back inside had been....well, he would not have to worry anymore.

Walter thought his hand would be shaking but he suddenly felt very calm. He was no longer afraid. The sense of relief felt blissful. He raised the gun to his head, closed his eyes and pulled the trigger.

*

The Angel station is on the Northern line of the London underground, in Islington. Now, the entrance is on the high street, Upper Street, but before the old station was modernised, the entrance and exit came out just round the corner at the top of City Road. There were traffic lights just outside, and a junction that lead to Goswell Road or St. John Street. If you wondered far enough down those busy streets, you would find several tall blocks of flats. These were the council estates that sprung up during the late 1950's and 60's.Behind every window, there is a story waiting to be told. Hundreds of families all with daughters, wives and mothers. This is the story of some of those girls who lived behind the windows. They are the Angel girls.

CHAPTER ONE   1958

Carrie Miller had been shocked the first time her Tommy had hit her. Not her darling Tommy! They had been together since their school days and had got married on her birthday, in June 1943. They had always had a volatile relationship, but in the beginning, it was Tommy's fiery personality that Carrie had found exciting. Tommy had a short temper but he had never been violent. Well, not towards her, anyway. She had seen him have a few fights with other boys at school, and he often clashed with his brothers, but he was very protective towards her, and had always treated her well. She had felt safe with Tommy by her side. She thought he would always protect her. When they had argued, they had always made up over a kiss and a cuddle.

Carrie Barlow, as she was then, had fallen for Tommy Miller the first time she had seen him. He had been the new boy in her class at school, a tall, dark haired lad with a cheeky grin, and a twinkle in his eye. They had both been twelve. All the other girls in the class had given Tommy the eye, but he had ignored all of them except Carrie. She had given him a shy smile, and he had grinned back at her. She had felt her heart give a little flutter. She never forgot that feeling, the first spark of love. He had asked to carry her books home and they had been inseparable after that. Carrie had felt very special. The handsomest boy in the whole school had singled her out! All the other girls were green with envy. Tommy had even had a playground scuffle with Gerald Dowelling, the tall blonde boy who kept smiling at Carrie across the classroom. Gerald had never looked her way after that, not after Tommy had blacked both his eyes. Tommy and Gerald had both been hauled into the headmasters study for that and had been given the cane for fighting, but Tommy had said it was worth it because Carrie belonged to him. He told Carrie that he was not going to let any other boy near her from now on. Carrie had not thought of Tommy getting into a fight as being possessive. At that tender age, such a thought would never have entered her head. No, she had been flattered. No one had ever shown that they cared that much about her before, let alone had a fight for her favour.

It was not exactly a romance at that age either but they both knew, even then, that one day they would get married. Carrie knew she would never look at anyone else. She had told Tommy that, and meant it after he and Gerald had their fight. Now she had her Tommy she would never look at any one else.

Poor little Carrie Barlow. Her fate had already been sealed.

They both left school at the age of fourteen, and Tommy had courted Carrie until they did get married, when Carrie turned twenty-one. It had been a long courtship, which was unusual for their part of London but they had waited because Tommy said they should save up, and get enough money to get a proper home together. He wanted to do things properly, he had said, and Carrie had felt proud that he cared so much. All of her friends had got married, and most had ended up living with their own mums or their in laws. Tommy had told her he wanted to wait until they could afford a nice little place of their own. Maybe a little house in the country somewhere, he had said dreamily, with a garden where he could grow vegetables and Carrie could plant lots of flowers. However, then the war came, and Tommy had proposed.

It had seemed so romantic to Carrie to be a war bride. Both of them decided they could not wait any longer to wed. Tommy had joined the army, but they had married before he had to join his regiment. Tommy had needed special permission. It had all seemed so exciting to Carrie. They only had one night together. Tommy had to join his regiment the very next day. Carrie still thought it had been the happiest night of her life.

Carrie had been a virgin, and her heart had thumped nervously when the two of them had finally been alone together, but her Tommy had held her, and made her feel so special, it had been wonderful.

All through the war, Carrie had waited faithfully, anxious for her Tommy to come home. She had written to him every week, telling him about life at home in London, and her time working in a munitions factory, and had waited fretfully for his replies, and his safe return. When the war was finally over, and Tommy had come home in one piece, Carrie had been ecstatic. In the days after the war, they had a passionate and exciting relationship. Tommy would take her out dancing, and they would come home tired but happy and make love until they fell into an exhausted sleep.

They lived in a tiny one bedroomed flat. It was in a tenement block. It was run down and there was one lavatory for the whole block, but it was all they could afford. Property was scarce and hard to come by.

Most of Central London had taken a savage beating from the bombing. The women did their best to keep their humble homes neat and tidy. Appearances counted and slovenliness was frowned upon. It was important to the women of London. No matter how poor they might be, there was no excuse for a grubby doorstep. The houses and flats were shabby, the landlord's never seemed to care about the property they rented out, but the women tried their best to make them look presentable. Windows may have been taped up to avoid the Germans shattering them with their bombs, but windowsills still needed polishing, and door mats were shaken regularly to get the dust out.

Tommy had five brothers, but Carrie was an only child, as her mother had died giving birth to her, and her dad had scarpered and left her to be brought up by his sister. Auntie Maud had done her best, and given Carrie food and shelter but not a lot of love. She had been a strict disciplinarian, and would use the strap on Carrie if she felt she had misbehaved, and sometimes would lock her in the coal shed. Carrie was a spirited girl though, and although she quickly learned how to behave in front of Auntie Maud, she was nobody's fool, and Tommy had loved her spirit and the fire that shone in her very blue eyes. She was wild, and Tommy wanted to tame her.

Tommy and his family had moved to Islington from East Ham, and their house was just a few streets away from where Carrie lived. Tommy's family had had to do a moonlight flit because they had not paid the rent on their house in East Ham. Tommy's dad worked hard, but his job as a painter and decorator did not pay too much, especially when most of his wages ended up behind the bar every Friday night.

The houses where Tommy grew up were always chaotic and noisy, and he and his brothers did not get on. Tommy's mother was not the sort of woman to be out scrubbing and polishing her doorstep. The family never stayed for too long in one house, because the rent did not get paid. Tommy's mother could not see the point in keeping the house nice when they never stayed put, and the kids had no respect for the property. Sometimes they stayed in the area, but word soon got round and landlords got suspicious and would not let them move in. Tommy's mum and dad did not see it as a problem; they would just pile their few belongings onto a handcart and find another house or rooms elsewhere. Tommy's dad would hear of a place to stay close to wherever his next decorating job was, and in the middle of the night, the whole family would quietly vacate the building and move into the next house. The Miller family were masters in the art of moon light flits.

There never seemed to be enough food to go round or enough shoes for all of the children. Their clothes were invariably hand me downs and usually shabby. Tommy had to fight for what he had, and fight he did. He was tall and strong, and he bullied his siblings mercilessly. He hated to look shabby, and he hated being hungry, so if he wanted a slice of bread and dripping or a shirt that was less scruffy than the rest he would fight his brothers for it. He and his brothers would build carts using planks of wood and old pram wheels, and take it in turns to ride round the streets. Tommy always had more than his fair share of turns though. He always got what he wanted. He had learned from an early age about survival of the fittest, and his brothers learned to stay out of his way and not argue if they wanted to avoid a thumping. Tommy had no qualms or conscience about taking what he wanted.

As soon as he was old enough to leave school, Tommy found himself a job in a factory and made sure he was never shabby or hungry again. He always gave half of his wages to his mum, he did not want his father pissing it up the wall, and he made his mum pay the rent. He was sick and tired of moving every few months, and he had met Carrie and was eager to stay put. Things looked good for a while, and Tommy was happy. He managed to keep a roof over their heads and for the first time in his life, he felt like he belonged somewhere.

Carrie had expected after her wedding that like most of her neighbours, she would soon be in the family way, and would have lots of babies to love and look after. She longed to hold her own child in her arms, and wanted so much to shower it with all the love that she knew she had inside her, just waiting to come out. She had never been given much love growing up, but she had a kind and gentle nature and she yearned for a child. She wanted her children to grow up secure, knowing they were safe and loved. She pictured herself pushing a pram proudly along the street, with a lovely little baby inside that was the apple of her and Tommy's eye. It never seemed to happen though. Each month that passed, Carrie would cry because she was not pregnant. There was an aching emptiness inside her, and Carrie always felt that something was missing in her life. She longed for the fulfilment of family life, and every time she saw a mother pushing a pram, she would feel the old familiar longing inside her, and have to fight back tears. It seemed so unfair. All around her, she saw women with too many mouths to feed who constantly shouted and moaned at their unwanted babies or gave them a hefty clout round the ear. She knew she would never do that if she were ever blessed with a child of her own. Her children would be loved, wanted, and taken care of everyday of their life.

As the months turned into years however, Carrie just had to learn to accept it, and she settled into a life of working hard. The doctor had told her there were no medical reasons why she could not conceive it was just one of those things. She had

11

worked at the munitions factory during the war. She trained as a precision engineer. There were no engineering jobs available for women once the war was over and the men came home however, so Carrie got an early morning cleaning job and tried to make the best of things. She was happy with her Tommy, he worked long hours but there was always food on the table. Tommy was not quite as affectionate as he used to be, and he seemed moodier somehow, but still, Carrie loved him. She reasoned with herself that things could not stay the way they had been during the first flush of love, and they jogged along together very well, she thought. She was content with her lot.

Although not having children was her own personal sorrow, Tommy did not seem to mind that they were childless. Carrie was, for the most part, content with her life. Tommy did not see much of his remaining brothers, they had moved out of London after the war. Only two of them had survived. His older brother, Stan, had copped it at Dunkirk and his younger brother Harry had died of dysentery in a prisoner of war camp. As for his brother Bobby, he had never been found. Their mother, Elsie, never seemed to get over the "missing in action" telegram. He too, had been at Dunkirk. Tommy's poor mother had died six months after the war ended. Tommy always said she died of a broken heart.

Tommy took his brothers deaths very hard, and his mother's death even harder. Carrie suspected that he felt guilty because he survived and his brothers had perished, but he would never talk about it, and got angry if Carrie brought it up, so she never did. Some- times Tommy would have nightmares and call out the name "Walter" but Tommy would not tell Carrie who Walter was. Tommy had not had a very close relationship with his father, who had liked a drink. Carrie knew that the family had been pushed from pillar to post because of his father's debts, and Tommy had longed for a settled home life. Carrie tried hard to give her husband the stability she thought he longed for.

Tommy did not shed a tear when his father died of cancer a year after he had buried his wife. His parents were buried side by side in Golders Green Cemetery but Tommy never visited their graves.

The months turned into years, and despite Tommy's dreams of moving into a nicer flat, or a little house in the country, they stayed in their two rooms. London was littered with bomb ruins and homes were like gold dust. Carrie did not really mind, she was just grateful to have a roof over her head. Many of her friends had been bombed out, and had been forced to go and stay with relatives. Some had not been lucky enough to even do that.

She still had nightmares about the air raids. She had lost a dear friend when the bombs had fallen on Dame Lady Owens School for Girls in Goswell Road. There had been a shelter there, but the bombs had hit a gas and a water main, and the poor souls seeking shelter had either been gassed, or drowned when the water main had shattered. Incendiary bombs had fallen that night on St Johns mansions, the block of flats in St John Street too. Women had rushed to the roof to put out the fires, and anyone who was available had run to help and try and dig out the trapped survivors seeking shelter beneath Lady Owens school in the next street. People had tried to dig out those that were trapped with their bare hands, but many perished.

Carrie thought often of her friend, Liza. She had worked alongside her in the munitions factory, and Liza always had a smile for everyone. She was just twenty-one. Her body had never been recovered. Carrie missed Liza's smiling face every day of her life. She had nightmares about her left buried under the rubble beneath the grounds of the school. It had been a harsh cruel war for so many Londoners.

One day Carrie realised her period was late. It was very late, and some quick calculations told her that she had not actually had the curse for two months. She was worried that she had begun an early change of life. She was thirty-five by then. When she had missed another period, she began to really worry, and decided that she ought to see the doctor. She had to ask Doctor Simmonds to repeat the news three times before she believed him, and then she still did not quite believe her ears. After fifteen years of marriage, she was pregnant.

Tommy put their names down for a new council flat when they found out that Carrie was expecting. Carrie was so excited. She had resigned herself to the fact that she would never be blessed with children. It had come as a huge shock to find out that at last she was carrying a baby. Tommy had been stunned when Carrie told him. They had lived in the two-roomed flat for fifteen years, but now they would need a proper home, he had said proudly.

There were many new blocks of flats going up in Islington after the devastation of the war. They had got lucky, and moved into a fifth floor brand new two bedroom flat just before the baby was born. The council had called it slum clearance, and the whole block they lived in was due to be re housed. It would take a while to re house all the tenants, but Carrie and Tommy were one of the first to move out.

Carrie had never been happier. The flat was so luxurious. It had two decent sized bedrooms, a bathroom and toilet, and even had central heating! There would be no more shivering for her anymore in the dark winter mornings. Carrie put pot plants on the windowsill of her little balcony, and could not wait until her new baby arrived. She had set to work right away, making it homely. She put aside a little money each week to buy things for the baby, and for the home.

It had all changed after baby Sarah was born. Carrie had called the baby Sarah because her friend Liza who had been so tragically killed in the air raid, had told her once that if she ever had a little girl she would call her Sarah as it was such a beautiful name.

Sarah Liza Miller came into the world with a mop of soft downy reddish blonde hair, bawling her eyes out. Carrie had enjoyed a trouble free pregnancy, with not even a hint of morning sickness, and a mercifully short labour. Her beautiful baby girl was placed screaming in her arms by the beaming midwife however, and for the first six months seemed determined to scream as much and as long as possible. When she was not screaming, She was still a fractious baby, and Carrie was always tired and on edge. It was difficult being a new mum for the first time at the age of thirty-six. No one was getting any sleep. Carrie had been so delighted to be a mother at last, and felt inadequate and guilty that she had not taken to motherhood like a duck to water. She had not been prepared for the overwhelming fatigue she felt, and the sheer hard work of caring for an infant around the clock. She tried hard, but it seemed like an uphill struggle. Tommy was becoming impatient with her, and it was making Carrie clumsy and easily flustered.

Tommy now worked as a drayman, delivering beer to all the local pubs. He had told Carrie whilst she was pregnant that now they finally had a baby on the way he needed to earn a decent wage and Carrie had been so proud of him when he had got the new job with the brewery. He loved his job. Unfortunately, he had discovered he loved the beer he delivered to all the public houses in the area, too. Carrie often thought he loved his Shire horses that pulled the dray carts more than he loved her. He spoke about them so animatedly. He did not have the same sparkle in his eyes when he spoke about her, or his only child. He worked hard, worked long hours, and always came home tired and stinking of the stables and beer. Tommy had always resented his father and his drinking as a boy. He could not see the irony in the fact that he was becoming just like the father he had disliked so much growing up. At first, he had excused himself by saying that all his work mates went for a drink after work. It was just a pint or two. Then as the pint or two became several, he said that a man was entitled to a drink after a hard day. Soon, he stopped making excuses at all, and told Carrie that he would do as he bloody well liked, and she could like it or lump it. Carrie did not like the new drunken Tommy. He changed when he had a drink inside him. He became like Jekyll and Hyde. That story had always scared her.

The row this time had started because she had moaned about the smell of booze and horses. She should have been used to the smell, of course, but it really bothered her now that the baby had arrived. The smell of the horses was bad enough, but the smell of the booze as Tommy lurched into the house and expected to be greeted with a big kiss and a cuddle was too much.

The brewery had a social club for its employees, and beer was very cheap. Tommy now went for a pint or two or three most days after work, and got into the habit of coming home blind drunk every Friday, which was payday. He was not a happy drunk. The more beer that went in, the nastier he got. He would pick arguments with his work mates, and when he eventually rolled home the worse for wear, nothing Carrie did or said was ever right. He also expected sex and Carrie found his beery breath and clumsy amorous advances repulsive.

Tommy was a brute when he was drunk. He turned nasty if Carrie refused him. She found it hard to understand his heavy drinking. Tommy had never been much of a drinker before the war. He had always said that his father's drinking had put him off. He had only started drinking when he came home when the war ended. He never talked about what happened when he was in the army, and away fighting, but he told Carrie that drinking helped him to forget. Sometimes he would have terrible nightmares, and wake up screaming, but he refused to tell Carrie what his nightmares were about.

Carrie had overheard him talking to his friend Frank. They had been in the same regiment together. She only caught snatches of their conversations. She had heard Tommy mention a young soldier called Walter. What had happened to Walter? Tommy always shut Frank up when he mentioned that name. Tommy refused to be drawn about his exploits during the war. Carrie did not push it; she thought the memories must be too painful for Tommy to relive. Tommy would sometimes scream Walter's name when he had bad dreams at night. Carrie had always been curious but was too afraid to ask.

The baby had not stopped crying all day; Carrie was exhausted and had burnt the steak and chips that Tommy had said he had been looking forward to all day. Steak cost a lot of money, he said, and now the silly cow had burnt it. They could hardly ever afford steak, and he liked it tender! How did she expect him to eat this fucking crap? It tasted like boot leather!

Sitting across the red Formica kitchen table with her own plate in front of her, Carrie had tearfully replied that it was only burnt because she had had to keep it warm for so long, if he had come home from work on time, it would have been just how he liked it. She added that he might try spending a bit less on beer and more on the housekeeping, and then they would be able to afford steak more often. Baby Sarah had only just gone off to sleep; Carrie's own dinner had grown cold whilst Carrie had tried to soothe the baby. She had finally closed her eyes and calmed down and Carrie had put her in her cot in the bedroom just minutes before Tommy had come home. The raised voices awakened her, and she began screaming again. "Can't you shut that little brat up?" Tommy shouted loudly, pushing his plate away from him.

Carrie was furious. "I've been trying to all bloody day!" she yelled, pushing her chair back and leaving the table to see to the baby. She paused before leaving the room and yelled, "Why don't you try if you're so bothered about the noise? After all, she is your daughter! You hardly ever even look at her! I'm worn out, and you don't do anything to help me with her!"

She had not expected him to lash out. He leapt from his seat with lightning speed. His fist caught her full in the face, and knocked her clean across the kitchen, falling in a heap on the red oilcloth. It was the shock more than the pain that made her cry out.

Carrie had sat, holding her throbbing face, shocked and sobbing on the kitchen floor. She expected Tommy to at least come and help her up, apologise even, and say he hadn't meant it, that it

18

would never happen again. If he had, she was sure she would have forgiven him, believed him. Maybe they could even have made it up in bed, or with a kiss and a cuddle, just like they used to. She would have over looked the blow and the smell of booze if only he had shown her a bit of the tenderness that she so longed for. Instead, she heard the front door slam, and he left her there, alone with the screaming baby.

He had not returned until the next day. Carrie assumed he had stayed with one of his few remaining friends. Probably Frank Gloucester. Tommy had merely glanced at Carrie's bruised face. He had not apologised, had not held her or looked remorseful.

After the first punch, it became a regular occurrence. Tommy would be fine for a while, and then something would set him off, usually after a drink or two, and crack! Another wallop. Tommy liked to win any argument. He would never settle for anything less. His way of settling things was to lash out.

Many times over the years that followed, Carrie thought about leaving, but where could she go? She had no family to turn to, even auntie Maud had died. She did not have a job she had given up working when Sarah was on the way, Tommy had insisted. He had said it looked bad if a pregnant married woman had to go to work. He did not want anyone saying that he wasn't man enough to look after his own wife. Tommy had control of all of their finances, and Carrie slowly realised that Tommy had control over every part of her life.

Gradually, over time, Carrie found herself accepting things the way they were. It was the only way she could cope. Her spirit became broken, and the fire in her blue eyes began to dim. She stopped arguing back, did not defend herself. Her self-confidence began to disappear, and with every slap, every bruise, she told herself that somehow it was her own fault; she must have provoked him in some way. She wanted to help him, Hoped that he would change, and Carrie felt sure that if anyone could help him, she could. She told herself every day that she still loved him. Carrie decided to devote her time to looking after her baby, and after the first difficult months, Baby Sarah blossomed into a beautiful little girl, who made life worth living for Carrie. She adored her daughter, and tried to make life as happy as possible for her.

Little Sarah was growing up into a pretty little thing; she had beautiful strawberry blonde hair and grey eyes and little dimples in her cheeks. She was a happy go lucky little girl and the bruises on her mums face and body were just a normal part of her everyday life. She had never known any different. Carrie put up with it. Tommy was her husband, and that was just the way it was. That was the only way she could get through each day. When he was sober, he was still her Tommy, and she still told herself over and over that she loved him. She wouldn't admit even to herself that she was afraid of the man she had married, even though every day now, she felt her heart constrict in fear as his key turned in the lock. No, she had made her bed, and now she had to lie in it. Auntie Maud had taught her that, and Carrie coped as best she could with her lot.

Carrie knew that the neighbours gossiped about her, she had seen them often enough exchanging looks in the lift when she had yet another black eye, but she tried her best to ignore them. She kept herself to herself, and concentrated on looking after little Sarah. She tried to shield her precious daughter from the violence as much as she could. It was not easy, but she tried her best not to do anything stupid to provoke Tommy when Sarah was around.

When Sarah started nursery at Compton Street primary school, Carrie had felt lost. To take her mind off it, she had found a little part time job, working in the sweet shop just along from Sarah's school. She knew that Cyril, who owned the shop, had a bit of a soft spot for her, but so long as Tommy never found out that Cyril fancied her, she felt that everything would be okay. Tommy had not been happy about her working, but Carrie had said that the money would be useful, she would still be home in time to cook dinner every evening and Tommy had grudgingly agreed. He swallowed most of their income each week in the boozer and he greedily thought of the extra rounds of beer Carrie's wages would buy him.

Carrie enjoyed serving the local children when they came in to spend their pocket money. She had even made friends with one of the mum's, Joycie, who brought her little daughter Suzy in to buy sweeties every Friday. Suzy was the same age as Sarah, and the two of them had quickly become friends too. Suzy had also just started in the nursery class. The two little girls had met in class waiting to take their turn on the rocking horse and had forged a friendship immediately. Cyril let Carrie pop out to collect Sarah from school, and Sarah would skip along to the sweet shop and spend ages choosing her sixpence worth of sweeties every Friday, with her new friend Suzy.

Carrie had started chatting to Suzy's mum at the school gates. Joycie Pond was the same age as Carrie and both their little daughters had started school on the same day. They had formed a tearful bond as they walked away from the classroom on that first morning. Carrie loved Joycie's happy go lucky nature. They had both laughed when they discovered they lived in the same block of flats, Brunswick Court. "Fancy us never bumping into each other until now!" Joycie had remarked.

Joycie had invited Carrie to her flat for a cuppa to take her mind off missing the girls.

Joycie had all mod cons in her flat. Carrie admired the shiny new radiogram in the living room, and the cocktail cabinet in the corner, near the serving hatch. "You should come to one of our parties," Joycie said cheerfully, as she poured out the tea, "We usually have a bit of a get together on a Saturday night. Me and Bobby love a bit of a dance! I dig out my Connie Francis records, and a bit of Elvis, and away we go!" Carrie smiled politely. She couldn't see Tommy wanting to go along to a party these days. Carrie did her best to keep him away from anywhere that had alcohol, and she could never relax in any social situation anymore. Tommy would always watch her like a hawk, and once they got back home, he would cross-examine her like a bloody police inspector, trying to catch her out. Of course, Carrie couldn't say any of this to her new found friend, so she made polite conversation and drank her tea.

Sarah had been delighted when her mummy had got a job in the local sweet shop. She was the envy of all her classmates. She loved to watch her mum serving the other children as she sat on the wooden counter eating her white chocolate mice and penny chews. Cyril was a grumpy sort of man, who didn't really seem to like children. Sarah often wondered why he chose to run a sweet shop if he didn't like children, but he was never unkind to Sarah, and was always nice to her mum. He would put her favourite white chocolate mice in a bag for her wink and say, "Here's a present from your uncle Cyril. Don't tell the customers"

Cyril told Sarah that she was beautiful, and looked just like her mother. Sarah had innocently told her daddy what Cyril had said when she went home that night.

Tommy had not been able to get it out of his mind. The more he thought about it, the more he realised that Sarah was the image of Carrie, and did not look like him at all. He had always thought it bizarre that after all those years of not having any kids Carrie had finally got in the family way.

What if the girl wasn't his? Sarah had bright carroty red hair. Where did that come from? He thought about it all night in the pub after work, brooding into his pints. Finally, he weaved his way home, getting angrier with every staggering step. By the time he put his key in the lock, he was incandescent with rage, but he wasn't going to let the bitch know it just yet. Let her stew, she would dig her own grave soon enough. How could he have been stupid enough to trust her? She must have been carrying on behind his back! He'd find out though, she would tell him. Oh yes, he would make sure of it. That fat old bugger Cyril in the sweet shop had an eye for Carrie. He wasn't daft, he knew he wanted to get his hands on his wife. He was as bald as a coot now, but Tommy wouldn't mind betting that he had red hair at one time. She would tell him, he would bloody well make her tell him.

Carrie was still up, and looked nervously towards the door, as Tommy filled the doorframe. She could tell by his face that he was in a bad mood, and her heart began to pound. She struggled to stay calm. Beads of sweat formed on her forehead and she began to tremble with fear. She waited for Tommy to say something. From experience, she knew it was better if she kept quiet, but he was just standing there, and his silence was terrifying. Finally, after what seemed like hours, he said just one word.

"Whore!"

It was pointless to argue. It only made him worse. Besides, she didn't want to wake Sarah up. Carrie didn't know who or what had put a bee in his bonnet this time. He had stood over her menacingly, and called her names, accusing her of all sorts of ridiculous things, saying that Sarah didn't look like him. He even accused her of sleeping with Cyril from the sweet shop. He was back to being the ruddy police inspector again. Who was Sarah's father, how many men had she slept with, what kind of a dirty, filthy slut had he married? On and on he went, quietly, menacingly. Carrie's head spun and she was too afraid to speak. He would not have believed her anyway, no matter what she had to say. She had stopped listening after the first punch. After the torrent of abuse, it had almost been a relief when he had finally struck her. It was usually safer to sink to the floor in submission. Usually he would give her a few slaps, a punch maybe and then leave her. He would go and fall onto the bed. He would be snoring in a drunken stupor within minutes. This time, however, Tommy had kicked her as she lay on the floor, and had only stopped when she had passed out.

Carrie had not been able to go to work in the sweet shop for several weeks. She had had to go to the hospital. Sarah had been very disappointed. She looked forward to going to the shop after school with her mum. Mummy had been ill with bruises again. Mummy often got ill with bruises. She didn't like it and tried hard to kiss them all better, but daddy would still shout and it scared her. She liked coming home from school with her friend Suzy, though. Suzy's mummy, auntie Joycie, was

24

kind and always smiling. So was Suzy's daddy, Bob. Auntie Joycie took her into the sweetie shop after school to buy chocolate mice until her own mummy got better.

Sarah had believed her mum would work in that sweet shop forever once she was well enough to return to work. Sarah loved it in the shop, loved all the huge glass jars on the dark brown wooden shelves, filled with their rainbow coloured sweets. She liked to drink in the smell of the toffees and the cough candy, and lemon bon bons, the humbugs and cola cubes. She loved the glass open topped counter, too, with its penny sweets, the white chocolate mice were her favourites but she loved the pink shrimps, and the black jacks and sherbet dabs too. Best of all though, Sarah loved Suki, the tortoiseshell cat, who picked her way carefully along the shelves, and sidled up close to Sarah for a tickle under her chin. Yes, Sarah though it was a wonderful place for her mum to work. If she were a good girl, her mum would let her help behind the counter. Sarah would stand carefully on the chair behind the wooden counter. She was learning how to use the little metal scoop and weigh out the big jars of sweets onto the scales, carefully pour the measured sweets into a paper bag and give the bag a twist before handing the bag over to the customer. Her mum would ring the money up in the cash register and let Sarah hand over the change. Sarah felt very grown up, and mummy and Cyril told her she was a very clever useful girl. Sarah had gone home beaming with pride and told her daddy that she had been useful. Daddy had told her to go and be useful somewhere else and had carried on reading his evening paper.

Carrie enjoyed her job too. When she returned to work after her bruises had faded it was a huge release for her. She hated being cooped up indoors, jumping at every noise, thinking

Tommy was coming home. It was stressful keeping little Sarah out of Tommy's way when he was at home. Carrie was terrified that Sarah would say something innocently, that would set him off again. Being in the sweetshop took her mind off things, and gave her a bit of dignity and independence. She too felt useful, and it was nice to have a bit of money to spend that she had earned herself. Her little bit of independence made it easier to cope with the stress of home. Tommy had not wanted her to go back to work in the sweet shop, he still was not totally convinced about Cyril, and had wanted to go and confront him. He had finally said he was past caring much to Carrie's relief, so Carrie had decided to risk returning to work. Life was so much more bearable when she had nothing more taxing to worry about than measuring out a quarter of lemon bon bons and a couple of liquorice boot laces for little Timmy Gregory spending his sixpence pocket money.

It was a tragedy when one night just after midnight, Suki the cat picked her way along the sofa in the flat above the shop and knocked over the ash tray that Cyril had carelessly left on the arm. A still smouldering cigarette butt set fire to the sofa, and within minutes, deadly thick grey smoke filled the flat. Very soon, the whole place was on fire. The shop burnt to the ground and Cyril had been found dead in his bed by the time the fire brigade arrived, lying beside his disabled wife May. The only one who got out alive was Suki the cat, who had disappeared through the bathroom window that had been left ajar. Suki was heard crying below the burning building by a neighbour, who took her in and made her very welcome after running to a call box and ringing for the fire brigade.

The neighbour was a non-smoker and a spinster. They both lived to a ripe old age, very happily together.

Carrie had been devastated. Especially when Tommy had laughed and said, he had never liked the old bastard Cyril anyway.

CHAPTER TWO

1977

Sarah Miller had grown into a beautiful young woman. She had long auburn hair, even though her mum still insisted it was strawberry blonde and bright grey eyes. She had left school in 1974, when she turned sixteen, and had managed to get a job as a check out girl in the Co Op on the estate where she lived with her mum and dad. It had seemed ideal at first, no fares or travelling to worry about, she could roll out of bed and be at work in five minutes. However, after a few months, Sarah was bored with the long hours and poor pay.

There was no one her own age to talk to and the manager was a dirty old man. Edna, the old biddy who worked on the other til, was past retirement age but refused to ruddy well retire. The moany old cow had the personality of an agitated wasp and the intellect of a walnut. All she did all day long was moan about "The youngster's these days" and tutted loudly after they left the shop. Edna was convinced than anyone aged thirteen to nineteen was a shoplifter, she never gave any young person the benefit of the doubt, including Sarah, and Sarah felt her beady eyes boring into her back all the livelong day. It was difficult because Sarah had to serve all the neighbours who had known her all her life and half of them expected her to slip them some groceries free of charge, or at the very least, give them extra Co Op savings stamps. It got very embarrassing when she said no, and quite a few of her neighbours had turned nasty, making snide remarks to her, or worse, to their friends in a loud stage whisper while they waited in the queue to be served. As if she was ruddy well deaf! She would have to sit and serve the other customers pretending she had not heard them, with her cheeks burning and fuming silently, knowing that beady-eyed Edna was watching and listening, and just waiting for her to slip up.

It had seemed like such a good idea to leave school. She wanted to be treated like a grown up, not a little kid, and could not wait to start earning money. She had spent the last year of school mucking about, really. Her and her best mate Suzy had had a good laugh at school. She thought wistfully of the days in the old science lab, with their decrepit old biology teacher, Mr Bunsen burner Turner. She could hear him now, yelling at them for using a sheep's trachea as a bookmark when they had been learning about the respiratory system. Suzy had sneakily slipped the windpipe into Sarah's book while she wasn't looking, just for a laugh, and Sarah had screamed in surprise when she had found it. The revolting thing had made a horrible mess of her exercise book. She and Suzy had then burst out laughing. Of course, Bunsen burner Turner had been on to them in an instant and a hefty detention had followed. At the time, it had seemed very unfair, but Sarah remembered it fondly. Poor old Mr Bunsen burner Turner. They had given him a hard time in those science lessons. They were never too naughty but did get up to some scrapes. All the equipment just seemed to be begging for a bit of misuse. Sarah missed her school days. The two girls had always been partners in crime, but had never done anything malicious. It was all mischief to make the boring lessons more interesting. There certainly was no one to have a laugh with in the poxy Co Op.

She had decided to look for another job, as she could not handle the endless boring days and the hassle from her customers expecting freebees. It was awkward telling Mrs Browning that no, she wouldn't slip those buns in her shopping bag when she knew she was likely to meet old Mrs Gravy Browning in the lift after work. Some of the ruder customers made snide comments because Sarah had gone to the Grammar school, Dame Lady Owens, and here she was, working in the Co Op.

Sarah did feel a bit ashamed if she was honest. Her mum had been so proud when she had earned a place at Lady Owens School. She had told Sarah all about her friend, who had been killed during an air raid and was buried on the site of the school. Sarah had been quite upset about it at the time. It felt a bit creepy. She never forgot poor Liza though. Her mum had given her the middle name of Liza as a memorial. There was a plaque up inside the school to commemorate the lost souls. Sarah and her mum had been in tears when they had seen it on the open evening before Sarah's first term. They had scanned the list of names and there she was, Liza Pennington. Never forgotten.

Sarah hated the smirking customers who thought that working in the Co Op was beneath a grammar school girl. "We thought you were meant to have brains", they would say chuckling, and thinking they were being really witty. They would look over at Edna, who would nod and tut and mumble that none of the youth of today had any brains, that was the trouble with this country. Sarah would grit her teeth whilst serving them, and try to smile politely. It was getting harder and harder to control herself, though. She badly wanted to lob tins of baked beans at Edna's head to stop her talking utter garbage and she was desperate to shut the old biddy up.

The manager, Mr Creepy creep from creepy town, had halitosis and leered down her top whenever he thought no one was looking. He was always watching her like a bloody hawk, too.

She had started to really regret leaving school. After a long day dealing with the rude customers and leering creep of a manager, sitting in a classroom with the smell of chalk dust and school dinner cabbage wafting over her didn't seem so bad. She even thought of old Bunsen burner Turner with affection now. She could have stayed on and sat her A levels, she had done reasonably well with her O levels. However, she had been keen to start earning some money, not just for herself but to help her mum out. Sarah liked treating her mum to a box of her favourite chocolates on payday, and buying her a new top now and again. Her mum had a lot to put up with. Dad had got worse over the years, and if Sarah could make her mum smile over a box of Milk Tray and remove the haunted look from her eyes for just a few moments, it was worth it. Well, most of the time. This job was terrible though, and Sarah longed for something better.

Just when she was beginning to think she would have to pole axe old Creepy creep from Creepy town with the giant economy box of cornflakes, after he had leered down her top once too often, her best friend Suzy had told her that there was a vacancy in Debenhams in Oxford Street.

Suzy had worked in Debenhams since she had left school. Sarah had been delighted, and applied at once. She had always loved shopping in Oxford Street, and loved going to Top shop with her mate Suzy. They would spend all day together trying on skirts, shoes and blouses, then crack up laughing pulling faces trying on hats and jewellery until they got told off by a haughty sale's assistant. They would giggle along the street and then when they had run out of money and energy, they would get the 73 bus back to the Angel, and walk home along Goswell Road. Suzy lived on the King Square Estate, and Sarah lived in Brunswick Court. Suzy and her family had lived in Brunswick Court when

Sarah and Suzy were both little girls, but they only had two bedrooms. When Suzy's brother, Robert was born they applied for a transfer and got a three bedroom flat on the new King Square Estate across the road. Sarah's mum, Carrie, and Suzy's mum, Joycie had met at the school gates when the girls first started school. Carrie used to work in the sweet shop just down the road from the girl's primary school. They had not even realised that they lived in the same block of flats. They were still friends, but Sarah's mum did not get out much to socialise these days. Her mum often told her about all the good times they had together back then, though. Carrie's eyes would light up as she described Joycie and told Sarah about her madcap antics. She sounded just like Suzy.

Sarah was thrilled when she got the job. It had felt wonderful to leave the Co Op knowing she never had to go to work there again. Edna had eyed her disapprovingly like an ugly little troll all day, and had kept muttering under her breathe about certain people getting idea's above their station. Mr Creepy Creep had given her a hopeful leer before she collected her things at the end of the day and said "How about a goodbye kiss?" she had looked appalled and said "How about a punch in the bread basket?" before flouncing off. She had not waited for the shutters to be pulled down. She walked away and did not look back.

She really liked her job in Debenhams. Sarah had not been able to believe her luck when she applied and had been accepted. She had been so relieved to be leaving the Co Op. It had many perks working in a posh department store in one of London's most fashionable streets. As well as being with her best friend all day it had a great staff restaurant, the food there was really tasty and cheap, she got a good staff discount and a decent wage. It meant that she could treat her mum much more often, and buy herself new clothes and makeup whenever she felt like it. Sarah felt privileged to have money to spend as she wished, and the days passed quickly. It seemed that she and Suzy hardly ever stopped laughing, and she really looked forward to going to work every day.

Sarah met Suzy every morning by Turnpike House, and the two girls would chat all the way along Goswell Road to the bus stop. The other girls who worked in Debenhams were mostly fun and friendly and up for a laugh, too. One or two of the madams in the cosmetic department were a bit stuck up, but Suzy called them the Pan stick people, and She and Sarah just ignored them, or played practical jokes on them when they got bored. They had to be careful of course, but so far had not been caught.

Sarah was just grateful she did not have to fend off Mr Creepy creep from creepy town anymore. Sarah could also go and have a browse round the other shops along Oxford Street during her lunch break if she wanted to. She and Suzy worked in the gift wrapping department, and spent all day wrapping presents and parcels in fancy paper, all tied up with coloured ribbons. The two girls had a large stand on the ground floor with a huge advertising board behind them that proclaimed, "Nimble fingers gift wrapping service. From a banana to a mini Cooper, you bring it, we will wrap it!" It was absolutely manic during the rush before Christmas, but for the rest of the year, they usually had a steady flow of customers, which made for a pleasant and not too hectic working day until the tourist season began in the summer.

Sarah and Suzy loved showing off their artistic flair with their elaborately wrapped boxes. 1977 was the year of the Queens silver jubilee, and their boss, Mr Michaelson, had shrewdly bought endless rolls of silver wrapping paper, and miles of red, white and blue ribbon. He had installed a bow-making machine on one corner of the counter, and taught the girls how to load the rolls of ribbon on to it, turn the handle and make endless bows in different colours. Sarah and Suzy would have a crowd of delighted tourists gather round their counter, watching the pair of them making bows, exchanging banter and wrapping patriotic presents with a flourish. As it got closer to the actual jubilee celebrations, the tourists were coming to London in their droves, and the steady flow of customers was getting to be an ever-waiting queue.

On the rare occasions when it was quiet and they had no customers, Mr Michaelson would send Sarah or Suzy to the men's wear section, to collect their empty shirt boxes. It was recycling at its very best long before recycling had even been invented. The men's wear department were glad to be rid of the boxes that littered the storeroom. The girls would fill their arms with the disguarded boxes and stagger back to the gift-wrapping counter. Then they would have to cover the old shirt boxes in wrapping paper to use as gift boxes. The boxes saved a lot of time when it got busy. The customer's purchases would simply be placed inside a tissue lined, covered shirt box and handed over.

Covering the empty boxes and their lids had been a tricky skill to master at first, and Mr Michaelson had spent a long time patiently showing Sarah how it was done. He had made it look very easy, and could cover a box and its lid in moments. Suzy was incredibly nimble, too, but had not been able to slow down enough to demonstrate how it was done to Sarah. It had taken hours of practise before Sarah could cover a box without the paper ripping when the shirt box lid was put on top. Now Sarah was a dab hand, and could expertly cover a box in a matter of minutes ready to use later. She enjoyed putting the finishing touches on the boxes, and making the bows and ribbon trimmings. While the two girls were busy wrapping and making bows, they would draw a crowd and it was great fun demonstrating and showing off a bit. They especially loved the American tourists who loved anything associated with the royal family. They loved the banter, and they tipped very well. Suzy and Sarah especially loved it when the pan stick people glowered over jealously at them as the customer's peals of laughter floated over towards the pungent perfume girls. The hapless pan stick people were always being sent out to squirt any unsuspecting customer with perfume and try to lure them to buy it. They hated it when Sarah and Suzy had customers and they had none.

Suzy spent a large part of her day flirting with any male customers, and often spent her tea break with the young sales men in men's wear. There were a lot of good-looking young fella's employed in Debenhams. That was another perk of the job. Sarah was a lot more discerning than her friend was, however. Suzy was always going out on dates with someone. So far, she had had dates with three blokes from men's wear, and one from the furniture department. There was also the memorable time last Christmas when the grotto was being set up, and Suzy had got chatting to the very youthful looking Father Christmas. Every lunchtime until the grotto opened to the public, Suzy had dragged Sarah into the grotto to talk with Santa. She had even sat on his knee and told him exactly what she wanted for Christmas. Suzy had been on several dates with

Santa over the festive period. She had laughingly told Sarah that Father Christmas had definitely come on Christmas Eve and had added with a grin that he had filled her Christmas stocking very nicely. Suzy often asked Sarah to tag along on a double date, and rather reluctantly, Sarah would sometimes oblige. Usually, Sarah's date would turn out to be only slightly better than Mr Creepy Creep from Creepy town, and Sarah would regularly threaten to strangle Suzy with the bow making ribbon.

When Suzy had been making merry with Santa she had tried to persuade Sarah to go on a double date with one of the Elves from the workshop. When Sarah had clapped eyes on him over the table at tea break, she realised that he really was Elf like, with ears like the F A Cup and a nose that could spear pickles. She had had to decline the kind offer, and had threatened to Staple Suzy to the grotto wall if she ever tried to fix her up with anyone ever again. At the moment, however, Suzy was without a date, and she was looking for her next conquest.

Apart from tagging along with Suzy, Sarah had not really got started with dating. The young sales assistants in the men's wear department were always asking her out, and one of the security guards had taken her for a drink one lunchtime, but Sarah was not interested in any of them. Her dad was very strict, and Sarah was not really looking for a boyfriend right now. If she was honest, men sort of scared her. Well, not scared her exactly, she was perfectly capable of thumping any lad who took liberties, but the thought of getting serious with a fella scared her.

She often pictured herself ankle deep in nappies, with screaming kids all around her, and a husband down the pub. The thought filled her with dread. As did the thought of ending up like her poor mum, living in fear every day, waiting and dreading a husband who came home and used his wife as a punch bag.

Sarah did not trust men very easily. She had grown up knowing that her dad could turn nasty at any moment, and she had learned to keep quiet and not upset him. Her mum often had bruises, and although her dad never hit her, well, not very often, she knew better than to upset him, because he would take his anger out on her mum when he thought Sarah was asleep.

Many a night over the years she had lain awake in her bedroom hearing the screaming rows through the paper thin walls, and she would cry silently into her pillow when she heard her dad finally silencing things with his fists yet again. She always wanted to go out and help her mum, but she knew better than to interfere. She had learned from bitter experience it would be her mother who would suffer if she did so.

Once, long ago she had bravely tried to stand up to her father after she had walked in on him slapping her mum around the face. She had screamed at him to stop and had shouted to him to leave her mum alone. She had told him she would call the police if he ever laid another finger on her mum. She had called him a bully and a coward and said he was not fit to lick her beautiful mum's boots. He had stood with his fists clenched while Sarah screamed at him, silent and looming in the doorframe. He had waited until she had finally finished her tirade. He had not said a word, waiting silently until Sarah had run out of steam. Then he had laughed in Sarah's face, slapped her one hard stinging blow across her cheek and turned to leave. He punched a big hole in the door and then slammed out of the house. Sarah had stood and let silent tears course down her reddened cheek. Her mother had rushed to her and Sarah had hugged her tearful mum then, not minding about her stinging face or pounding heart, thinking they had won.

Much later, he had returned, reeking of stale beer and had dragged her poor mum from her bed and beaten her to a pulp. He told Carrie that if Sarah ever interfered again, he would kill the pair of them. Sarah had had to admit defeat to protect her mother. Carrie had begged her not to interfere again. Sarah had given in, sitting and sobbing in her dark bedroom, covering her ears trying to blot out the terrible sounds. She hoped in her heart that one day the horrible old bastard would get what he deserved. Her dad had never hit Sarah again though. Sarah had made that perfectly clear. Her father had flown into many rages as the years passed and her father had tried to raise his fist to Sarah once more. She had quite literally stood up to him and said bravely "Hit me and you had better watch your back! I promise you, one day I'll get my own back. You won't know where or when, but I'll bloody make sure you get what you deserve!" Tommy had laughed at her, but he had never raised his hand towards his daughter again.

Tommy had punched another hole in the door instead. Her poor mum's life was constant drudge and fear. Sarah could never understand why her mother put up with it, and even made excuses for him. Carrie would say that Tommy still had bad dreams about the war; he had had a terrible time of it. He would call out Walter, his friends name, during the night. "He has a lot of things going on in his head," Carrie would say to Sarah, as if that excused the rages he flew into. Sarah was determined that she was not going to make the same mistakes. She was quite content to carry on working in Debenhams, having a laugh with her best mate Suzy. Sarah smiled to herself remembering the mad things they got up to when they got bored at work.

One morning when it had been quiet at work, Suzy had put two enormous round beads down her tight fitting tee shirt, right where her nipples were. She had undone her work overall and pointed her prominent features at Sarah. Sarah had nearly choked trying not to laugh at the peanut smuggling that was going on under her friend's clothes. "I dare you to go and ask Pervy Patrick in the men's underwear section for empty boxes like that," Sarah said, after she had managed to compose herself. Having exhausted supplies from the men's shirt department, the girls had recently had to expand their scrounging departments. "Only if you come, too" Suzy said, winking. Sarah smiled. She knew Suzy could never resist a dare.

The two girls put their Back in five minutes sign on to the counter and walked off. This was a sign they had made themselves, and was only to be used in dire emergencies. Their boss definitely did not approve of leaving the department in pairs, but sometimes rules just had to be broken. Besides, they knew that Mr Michaelson was away on a managerial course, and Miss Parish was on her tea break. They decided to risk it, and hoped that the Pan Stick people would not grass them up when Miss Parish got back from her break.

Pervy Patrick was a tall thin wisp of a man of about forty-five. He had a very prominent Adams apple that bobbed up and down alarmingly whenever he spoke. He looked as if he had swallowed a small rodent that was now frantically scrabbling in desperation to escape. He was of course married; the creepy ones nearly always were, with several children left no doubt squalling at home with their poor wives. Pervy Patrick always seemed to be either at work or in the pub across the road after work leering at the young office girls. Sarah and Suzy wondered if his poor kids even recognised him when he got home. They only knew he was married with a family from talking to his long-suffering work mates. They had met the poor woman once at the annual Christmas party. He thought he was God's gift to all of the young girls who worked in the department store. He had a most unfortunate habit of never looking at any girl's face. Instead, he stared fixedly at their bosoms, with an odd leer on his greasy face. He always wore a shiny suit with a kipper tie, and had an air of oiliness about him that was quite frankly, repulsive. His over powering aftershave was, Suzy was convinced, called O'De repugnant. Suzy had made up a mock commercial about his aftershave. Sarah would cry with laughter, sitting in Suzy's bedroom as Suzy pretended she was on the telly. In her best pan stick people voice, she would hold up a bottle of her dad's aftershave and say, "Do you need a woman repellent? Squirt yourself liberally with Pervy Patrick's O'De Repugnant, it works every time!"

Patrick Dunstan's face lit up like a row of fairy lights as he saw the two girls from the gift-wrapping stand approach him now. He had convinced himself that the one called Suzy fancied him. He smoothed down his kipper tie and hoped the girls would not notice the gravy stain on it. The two girls came to his department on the flimsiest of excuses. As the girls got within earshot, he heard Suzy say to her friend "My, it's a bit nippy round here today"

Suzy and Sarah had had to disappear into the staff toilets to compose themselves afterwards. They knew they would probably get into trouble, as Miss Parish would surely have noticed them missing by now, but this was an emergency, and they would face the wrath of Miss Parish if need be. Sarah was actually crying with laughter, and dabbed at her eyes with a bit of toilet paper. "Oh my God!" she said when she had regained the power of speech, "Did you see his face? I thought his eyeballs were gonna pop right out of his head! And that lump in his neck had a life of its own!"

When the girls got back to the gift-wrapping counter, Suzy was minus her beads. There was quite a queue of customers, but Miss Parish was nowhere to be seen. They could both feel the waves of loathing wafting across from the Pan Stick people, but that was nothing new. Secretly, they both felt that Miss Parish had a bit of a soft spot for the pair of them, as she was never very hard on them.

Miss Parish was the ultimate professional, and was excellent at her job, but she had a human touch and the girls knew she had a sense of humour. They respected her for that. They got the impression that Miss Parish disliked the Pan Stick people as much as they both did. They loved to tell tales and Sarah and Suzy could often hear their whinny voices bending poor Miss Parish's ears over the makeup counter.

Suzy asked Sarah over their lunch if she fancied going to a Rock and Roll revival dance that was coming up at the Lyceum. Suzy looked up expectantly at Sarah, swallowing a chunk of meat and potato pie, and spearing her next mouthful on to her fork. Sarah nodded eagerly. She loved dancing, and the rock and roll dances were great fun. She knew that Suzy would be on the lookout for a new fella, but what the hell. She hoped her dad would not stop her from going. If he were in a bad mood, he would moan at her mum and say that she encouraged her to go out flirting with boys. Sarah's dad did not like her hanging around with boys. He still treated her as if she was twelve. It sometimes made life at home a bit tense. It was good to have a bit of light relief at work, and she had a great time relaying their latest antics to her mum when she was at home and her dad was out. She did not really care that her dad ranted if she ever had a date. She was used to it. He ranted about a lot of things, and always had. She told herself she was not ready to settle down, and had no desire to get herself tied to some brute of a man the way her poor mum had done. Even though she was now nearly nineteen, she had only ever been on a few dates, mainly to keep Suzy happy, and had never met a fella who she wanted to see again. She knew that her dad would not be happy if she had a steady boyfriend, so it was just as well that she did not have anyone in mind.

She had had her fair share of schoolgirl crushes of course, on a few local boys, and had plastered her bedroom walls when she was younger with photos and posters of Marc Bolan and David Cassidy, that she saved from her Jackie magazines, but there had been no one special in real life yet. She remembered when she had gone to a school dance once with Suzy. She had seen a boy from Sir Philip Magnus School. His name was Jimmy Perkins and he was five foot ten inches of gorgeousness. He had made Sarah's heart flutter, all right. She had looked longingly at him all night, hoping he might ask her for a dance, and try to get to know her better, but he never did. She would see him around sometimes; he lived near Exmouth Street market. Sarah had always been too shy to speak to him. She had made her mind up to at least catch his eye and smile at him the next time their paths crossed. However, when the next time did come, it had been raining and Sarah was soaked to the skin and looked like a drowned rat. Of course, she had left her umbrella on the bus that day. Her hair always did inexplicable things whenever it was humid. She had caught sight of herself in a shop window and had been afraid. Very, very afraid. The rain had soaked up her trouser legs and reached her knees. Her hair looked like an unkempt bush that badly needed pruning and her jacket was splattered in mud. The same bus that had driven off with her umbrella still on its seat had kindly done the mud splattering as it departed. She had tried to duck out of sight before Jimmy Perkins spotted her. It was too late. He walked past her and grinned at her mortified expression. She never did get to know Jimmy Perkins.

Sarah smiled remembering the way Suzy always fell head over heels with every boy or member of a pop group she thought was good looking. Sarah remembered the time when she and Suzy had still been at school, and Suzy had asked Sarah to help her cover her bedroom ceiling in posters of Slade. Suzy was mad about the group and loved Noddy Holder the lead singer, and Jimmy Lea the bass player. She had been collecting pictures for absolutely ages. They had spent hours up a stepladder, armed with rolls of sellotape, listening to and singing along to Slade singing "Cum on feel the noize" and when they had finished, the entire ceiling was covered. There was not a single gap to be seen. When they had finished, the pair of them fell exhausted on to Suzy's bed, and lay on her candlewick bedspread looking up to admire their handy work, and forget their aching arms and necks. Suzy had wanted to look up at Noddy Holder and Jimmy Lea whilst she lay on her bed and see them when she woke up every morning. They were even too tired and achy to take the record off the turntable of Suzy's Dansette record player.

 It was less than a week before the sellotape began to peel away, and Suzy said it frightened the crap out of her when

Noddy and Jimmy fluttered down in the middle of the night and landed on her face. She had screamed blue murder, and her dad, Bob, had come running in to her bedroom, closely followed by her mum, Joycie, carrying her pillow in her arms, thinking Suzy had an intruder in her room. Suzy's dad had grinned at Suzy's mum, and mumbled "what were you gonna do if it had been a burglar you silly mare, tickle him to death with the feathers from yer pillow?"

Sarah made sure her mum took some money for her keep each week, and had shrewdly opened up a savings account for herself. She enjoyed spending what was left over. She and Suzy spent most of their wages on clothes, records and make up, and, when her dad allowed her out, going to the disco to dance the night away. Sarah was happy to dance with the boys that asked her, but if they wanted to take things further, or asked her out on a date, so far she had nearly always refused. She was far from timid, though. Her father scared her, but she was afraid for her mother's safety, not her own. She kept the peace at home and did as she was told only to save her poor worn down mother from yet another good hiding.

As she got older, she was finding it harder and harder to hold her tongue. She longed for the day when the miserable old bastard got what he so richly deserved. Sarah had just convinced herself that fella's that made your heart race and violins strike up in the Technicolor sunset of life only existed between the pages of slushy romantic fiction. She did not think it ever actually happened in real life.

Sarah would have loved to leave home, and do a flat share with Suzy. She was young and it was an exciting time to be living in London. They had talked about it often enough, but even if they could have afforded it, Sarah knew she could never leave her mother at the mercy of her father. For the time being, she bided her time, and was content to enjoy herself at work, and go out dancing with her mate whenever she could afford it. She was still waiting to meet a bloke who would knock her socks off, and make her want to dance with him for the rest of her life. She thought she would be in for a very long wait.

"Mum, can I borrow your ruffled petticoats to wear on Saturday night? There's a fifties rock and roll revival dance on at the Lyceum. Me and Suzy haven't been to one of those for ages! It sounds like a laugh. Do you think Dad'll mind if I go?" Sarah was helping her mum with the washing up after dinner. Tommy was in the living room, with his feet up watching football on the telly.

"I'm sure he will let you go, love. Just pick your moment to ask. Course you can borrow my petticoats. Huh, it's not as if I'm ever gonna use em again! Blimey, that takes me back! I used to go out dancing wiv yer dad, yer know. Don't look so surprised, love! He was quite a groover in his day! I loved a bit of a dance...I'm still a bit in love with Buddy Holly"

Suzy Pond admired her appearance in her full-length bedroom mirror, twirling this way and that to get the full effect. She was meeting her best mate Sarah in a few minutes, and they would be off to catch their bus to go to the Lyceum. There was a special dance on this evening, a 1950's style rock and roll dance and all the girls that went dressed up in 1950's outfits got in free. Suzy and Sarah loved going to these fifties dances but had not been to one in ages. They always had a good time. Teddy boys were back in style now, and although neither she nor Sarah particularly liked the greased back hair the boys wore, and the whiff of Brylcream that went with them, they both loved the music and the dancing. Some of the boys wore American style fifties clothes with high waist pleated trousers, and bowling shirts, and they were dead sexy. They did not wear their hair greased back, they kept it short and tidy, just how Suzy liked it. She liked to run her fingers through a man's hair without her fingers getting stuck in greasy goo. That was a real turn off for her. She was really looking forward to her night out. She had spent age's glamming herself up. Preparing for a big night out was half the fun.

Suzy was wearing her mum's beautiful green and white original fifties dress, with its matching bolero. She had carefully put on layers of stiff white petticoats underneath, and had curled her hair. She had tied her long dark hair up in a ponytail, and had tied a green ribbon in her hair. Her ponytail swung beautifully as she turned her head to check it looked right. She had bobby socks and little lace up pumps on her feet, in the American style she loved. She thought she looked the bee's knees. She had her mums original 1950's handbag with its baker light handle to complete her ensemble. Finally, she put on her pale pink lipstick and winked at her own reflection. "Blimey, those teddy boys will be lucky tonight!" she told herself in the mirror. Then she laughed, and hurried off to meet Sarah.

The noise from the stage pulsated through the Lyceum, and really hit them as soon as they reached the dance floor. Sarah could feel the vibration of the music through her feet, and her ears were beginning to hurt, which was always a sign of a belting good night. It was not yet 9'0 clock, but was already crowded. The Dee Jay was up on the stage, head phones on and totally lost in his choice of music. Big Bopper's Chantilly lace was blaring out, and couples were jiving. Sarah looked around excitedly, trying to drink it all in. She loved watching other couples dancing. Some of them were amazing, and looked really athletic. Good jiving was an absolute art form. Everyone had made a real effort and there were some fabulous outfits.

The teddy boys had suits on in every colour of the rainbow, with shoes to match their suits, and the girls all had their best jiving dresses on, or blouses and swirly skirts. Some of the girls had short scarves around their necks, or tied in bows in their hair. One or two boys were dressed in the American style and Suzy was casually trying to steer Sarah towards them.

Sarah could not help but smile. She thought that Suzy looked incredible. Her outfit was stunning and her hair looked beautiful tonight. She always did look spectacular, though, Sarah thought. Suzy was a very pretty girl, with a cheeky smile and mischievous blue eyes. Her dark hair shone under the glitter balls hanging from the dance floor and Sarah knew it would not be long before some bloke would come over and claim a dance. Sarah let herself be guided closer to the boys she knew her friend had been eyeing up. On a night out with Suzy, Sarah was content to go with the flow.

Sarah herself had on an electric blue dress with a flared skirt that she had found a few years ago in a vintage clothes shop. The skirt had a print of little poodles around the hem. Poodles on fabric and jumpers were the height of fashion in the 1950's. Sarah had spotted several poodle designs swirling around on the dance floor. With her mum's petticoats underneath it, her own full swirly skirt swished wonderfully when she moved. She too had her hair tied in a ponytail, and had curled the ends, and she had on bobby socks and lace up pumps. She had thought about wearing her mum's stiletto shoes, as they both wore the same size. She had practised wearing them, but although walking was fine, she worried she might break her ankle or neck if she attempted jiving in those killer heels. She could manage to balance beautifully wearing her platform sole shoes whilst dancing at a normal disco, but jiving was a totally different skill. She was a bit concerned that her mum's stiletto might have come flying off her foot mid jive, and impale a teddy boy on the dance floor.

The Big Bopper had finished, and Buddy Holly began singing "I'm a gonna tell ya how it's gonna be…" two teddy boys, in full brothel creepers and drain pipe trousers, sidled over. "Fancy a dance, darling?" One of them whispered in Sarah's ear. Before she had time to reply, she found herself being whisked away, and twirled around. She could hear Suzy giggling at her, as, skirts flying, she flew through the air and landed non too daintily before being pulled through the legs of her new found dance partner.

After two more songs, Sarah had to beg for mercy, as she needed a rest and to get her breath back. Jiving was more exhausting than any exercise class at the gym. One of these days if she wasn't careful Sarah feared a slipped disc at the hands of a teddy boy. "Okay sweetheart. " Said her teddy boy amiably, "see you later, maybe" He shuffled off, and disappeared into the crowded throng. She could see Suzy, still twirling with the other teddy boy, but even Suzy had to come up for air, and after Elvis finished Jail house rock, she too had to admit defeat. They both headed for the bar to get a well-earned drink. As they each sipped a long tall glass of lemonade to quench their thirst, it was as if Suzy had read Sarah's mind as Suzy said "They should supply a physiotherapist at the bar, I think I've put my back out" her voice trailed off and she nudged Sarah in the ribs. "Ooh, look, I've just spotted James Dean!"

Sarah followed Suzy's gaze and saw a young blonde man propping up the bar, surrounded by a group of friends. He did, indeed look like James Dean. Sarah had always had a soft spot for James Dean. She had loved him in Rebel without a cause. She couldn't stop staring at the Jimmy Dean look alike at the bar.

He had shiny blonde hair and was wearing a pair of smart dark blue, high waist pleated trousers. He had a powder blue American style-bowling shirt. Sarah had to admit he looked very handsome. He looked over at Sarah and smiled. Sarah felt her heart jolt. That smile had suddenly made fireworks appear for Sarah. She could not help herself she smiled back. Wow! She thought. Sarah actually felt her pulse begin to speed up. Now here was a bloke she could finally get excited about, she told herself. He was really gorgeous! Hello there Mr Gorgeous gorgeousness from planet Gorgeousness, she told herself. He was definitely the sort of fella that her dad would not approve of, but suddenly Sarah didn't care. Maybe the slushy romance novels had a point after all. Even Jimmy Perkins hadn't made her feel quite like this. Sarah sighed happily, and whispered to Suzy "Ooh, I want him"

Suzy grinned at her friend in surprise. "Well, it's about time, I must say! Let's go get him for you, then.."

However, just when the girls were trying to figure out a way of casually getting closer so he would speak to them, a pretty, dark haired girl appeared by his side, wrapped her arms around his neck and kissed him full on the lips.

Suzy put her empty glass down in disgust, and dragged Sarah back onto the dance floor for another dance. Sarah had never felt less like dancing in her entire life. She was bitterly disappointed.

Jonny Mason was not happy. Damn that stupid Louise! Why did she have to come over and spoil things just when he had spotted the most gorgeous girl he had seen ever? Louise Blakely Green, a pretentious name for a pretentious stuck up spoilt brat. He wondered incredulously how many years of oppression and excessive school fee's it had taken to turn Louise into the upper middle class snobbish spoilt brat that she was. He couldn't stand her, but she followed him around like a bad smell. She was much too young for him, anyway. She was still at school, for Christ sake. Jonny was twenty-two, nearly twenty-three, and had come back from university and was for the time being, working with his dad in his dad's antique shop. The shop specialized in antique toys, and despite himself, Jonny was really enjoying going to auctions and antique fairs up and down the country with his father, and learning the trade. He had studied history at university, but had left with no real plans for his future career. He had only intended working with his dad for a stopgap, but much to his surprise he was loving every minute of it.

Louise was the daughter of one of his dad's business friends, and had been trying to get Jonny interested in her for ages. Jonny had not seen Louise for years, but she had been hanging around him ever since he had come home from Uni. She was like a ruddy wasp the way she buzzed round him all the time. Right now, he would have given anything to swat her away and flick her out of his life forever.

He had been really annoyed when she appeared as if by magic, here tonight. Dad must have told her he was coming. He vowed to throttle his dad later, the blabbermouth! He had quickly disentangled himself from Louise, made his excuses and gone on the prowl to try to find his mystery girl, but she was nowhere to be seen. He was just about to admit defeat, when he spotted her out on the dance floor, jiving with a bloke in a lime green suit.

She certainly knew how to dance. He stood, mesmerised, watching her move as Mr Lime Green twirled her around and lifted her high into the air. As "That'll be the day" ended, he seized his chance, and stepped in before the jiving citrus fruit had time to ask her for another dance. "Can I have a turn with the twirling?" he asked her, smiling into her eyes. Mr Lime stepped aside graciously.

She had the most beautiful eyes. She gave him a shy little smile, that immediately did funny things to Jonny's insides and then they began to dance. Jonny silently sent a thank you to the Dee Jay as the jiving songs gave way to Sealed with a kiss. As the music slowed down, Jonny held his dream girl close and never wanted to let her go. The mere nearness of her was sending his pulse rocketing. He tried to ask her what her name was above the roar of the music, but he could not hear her reply above the noise. Did she say Zara? He drank in the lovely clean fruity shampoo smell of her hair that was the colour of polished copper, and the closeness of her ivory skin. He snuggled in as close as he dared to the nape of her neck. He longed to kiss her beautiful soft skin, but did not want to take liberties. They did not speak again during the slow song. He would have to let her go to hear a reply, and he wanted to hold her in his arms for as long as he could. Sealed with a kiss ended and Buddy Holly was back, singing, "It's raining in my heart" Jonny was relieved that this vision of loveliness seemed happy to carry on dancing. Jonny desperately wanted to see her again, and needed to know if she felt the same way. "Do you live far?" he whispered into her ear.

"Not very far, near the Angel" she whispered back. "Oh, that's fantastic, I've just...."

The song finished, and Jonny would have been quite happy to carry on dancing, so long as he could be with her, but the gorgeous girl's friend had surfaced and interrupted Jonny mid-sentence. The girl gave him a wistful little smile that made Jonny's heart melt but she said she had to go. Her friend, a bubbly looking type, was pulling her away. Jonny wanted to object, but it was too late. That was it, she disappeared into the crowd, and Jonny, feeling like a complete twerp, could do nothing but fight his way back to his mates at the bar. He kept looking for her for the rest of the evening, but she did not reappear.

It was Thursday morning, and Sarah could not wait for it to be lunchtime. It had been so slow; she was running out of things to do to look busy. They had only had one customer so far. She wondered where all the tourists were today. She had already been to the men's wear department and collected all the empty shirt boxes. She and Suzy were taking as long as possible to cover them in silver wrapping paper. They had made so many bows with the bow maker that they were running out of ribbon.

Miss Parish was on the prowl, and although she was not that bad, she would probably find them something horrible to do if she saw them standing around doing nothing. She may have had a soft spot for the girls on gift wrap, but even she had a job to do, and she couldn't pass by and say nothing if they appeared to be slacking. Sarah hoped Miss Parish would not send one of them to the stock room for more ribbon. She was terrified of that stock room. The last time she had ventured in, she had seen a cockroach. It had been so enormous she swore to Suzy when she had stopped screaming that she could have saddled it up and rode it home.

They had nearly run out of boxes to cover, and had polished the counter and straightened the display endlessly to look busy. Now they had resorted to tearing up tiny pieces of black card and sticking them over their teeth and smiling at the disgusted girls from the cosmetics department to amuse themselves. The pan stick people were not amused, of course, and Suzy had heard one of them say "How childish!" to her equally stuck up friend.

 "Oh my god, I don't believe it, it's him!" said Suzy excitedly, as Sarah bent down to get yet another shirt box to cover. Suzy quickly spat out her cardboard decaying dentures. "What?" said Sarah distractedly, searching for the lid to the shirt box she had picked up. They had covered the best boxes and all that were left now were the stragglers, the ones that had somehow managed to separate themselves from their matching lids. She began coughing. She had almost swallowed her own black cardboard. "James Dean! From the Rock and Roll dance! Over there, look!" Suzy had felt really guilty for dragging Sarah away from the James Dean look alike. Sarah had confessed that she had really fancied him. The two girls had looked for him when they had finished in the ladies room, but when they had finally seen him; the eager looking young girl had her arms around him again. Sarah had been really disappointed and had made Suzy hide away at the other end of the dance floor for the rest of the evening. It had been physically painful watching him with another girl. She had had an almost irresistible urge to go over and rip the other girls head off.

Sarah popped her head up from below the counter like a Meer Cat on lookout duty. She scanned the shop floor eagerly. Oh sweet mercy, It was him all right! And he was heading their way!

In the cold light of day, he looked, if it was possible, even more handsome than Sarah had remembered, and the girl he could not seem to shake off at the dance had miraculously disappeared. Sarah was surprised to feel her heart begin to thump. She had always held back where boys were concerned, and so far had had no trouble in doing so. What was it about Jimmy Dean here that had got her all of a lather? She could have killed Suzy at the dance when she dragged her away after James Dean had asked her for another dance. Suzy had been desperate for the loo, and they always went to the ladies room together when they were on a night out. It was an unwritten rule; girls went in pairs to spend a penny. Sarah had looked for James Dean when they had come back, but was bitterly disappointed when she had spotted him at the bar, with the pretty young looking girl hovering around him again. She had told Suzy that she wasn't bothered though, and they had gone to dance at the other end of the dance floor, well away from the bar. She hadn't told her friend that she had a pain in her heart at the sight of him with that other girl. She didn't like that feeling. It made her feel vulnerable, and she wasn't falling into that trap. She didn't think she would ever see him again, but here he was, large as life and twice as handsome.

He was now standing just a few feet away, and Suzy was smiling so hard in his direction that the glare from her pearly whites could easily have dazzled and brought down a light aircraft. Suzy was definitely not shy when it came to boys. She would do anything for attention. Sarah wished that Suzy had still been wearing her blacked out teeth. She just stood and tried to look busy. She couldn't think of anything else to do. "I'll give you all of next week's wages if you let me serve him!" Suzy hissed as he strolled closer. "I'll find out if he and that young trollop are an item for ya!" Sarah did not have time to argue.

James Dean had totally ignored Suzy and her dazzling smile, much to Suzy's disgust, and had asked Sarah if she would wrap up a tankard he was holding. He had been sent to collect it for a friend of his father, it was a birthday present from his wife, he added, unnecessarily. As Sarah picked out a box for it, she could feel her heart fluttering. She struggled to compose herself, and hoped Mr Gorgeous from the planet Gorgeousness wouldn't notice the effect he was having on her. She told herself to get a grip, and proceeded to wrap the rather naff tankard in gold paper. Suzy desperately tried to muscle in and start a conversation.

" Didn't we see you at the Lyceum, at the rock and roll dance last weekend?" she said sweetly. She noticed that James Dean couldn't take his eyes off of Sarah, but he looked over at her when Suzy spoke. "So it was you two! I thought you looked familiar!" he said as casually as he could. He wasn't very good at faking things. "Did you both have a good time?" Sarah, still with her head down and wrapping the parcel, said pointedly "You certainly seemed to be having a good time with your girlfriend. I saw her all over you after you asked me for a dance."

"Girlfriend?" He said looking genuinely puzzled. Then the penny dropped. Bloody Louise again! "Oh, did you see me with young Louise? Silly little girl wearing a bright pink dress?" Suzy nodded. Sarah pretended not to care. "She definitely is NOT my girlfriend. She's like a pesky wasp, I just can't seem to swat her away… but I promise I'm free as a bird! She wants to be my girlfriend, though. Got a bit of a crush on me, so I've been told." He winked and grinned as Sarah's head shot up, and added, "She's got no style, though, not like you two…." Sarah had finished his parcel, and slid it across the counter. She smiled her best sales girl smile and said as casually as she could "There you go, sir. That will be fifty pence please" He took the present, but didn't move. He was persistent, Sarah thought, I've got to give him marks for trying. She had to admire his courage; he wasn't a bit put off by her aloof face. Her heart was now doing somersaults, and was thinking of joining the acrobatics troupe in the circus. She wondered what the snotty tarts from the cosmetics counter would say if they saw her lasso this gorgeous specimen with the Royal blue ribbon and hold him hostage under the counter until closing time.

He took some money out of his pocket, and placed it on the counter. Sarah rang his purchase up on the cash register and gave him back his change. She tried her best to avoid eye contact, but his amazing blue eyes were like magnets, and seemed to be pulling her in. She still tried to maintain an air of distain, but it wasn't easy. His eyes were like sapphires.

He was really quite magnificent. Their fingers touched as he held out his hand to take his change. Sarah felt a tingle like an electric shock jolt her body, and she half expected her teeth to light up and send sparks of lightening across to the Clarins counter. She hoped it would zap little Miss Pan Stick who was goggling over at Mr Gorgeousness. Sarah was jolted back to his remarkable twinkling eyes, as he began to speak again. He had a wonderful soft hypnotic voice.

"I take it that you are interested in fifties music? Do you like classic cars at all? You know, from the same era? Only the Chelsea cruise is on this weekend, I wondered if you would like to go with me?" he was well spoken, but not too posh. He definitely wasn't a cockney, though. Sarah wondered idly if he could hear her heart, as it was now pounding so loudly it sounded like the percussion section of the Andy Ross orchestra, the band that played live at The Lyceum most Saturday nights. Buggering Bognor! Had her lugholes deceived her? Or had he just asked her out on a date?

Sarah could see Suzy practically jumping up and down in excitement out of the corner of her eye, like a hyperactive puppy dog. She ignored her. "Cruise?" she said, pretending to look puzzled. She didn't want to appear too eager. "I'm not going on no cruise. I get sea sick in the bath." A little smile played at the edge of her lips but as the words left her mouth, she wished with all her heart that she could reel them back in again.

Bugger! Bugger! why did I say that? Sarah told herself crossly. He would think she wasn't interested. It was all right though. He laughed, exposing a set of neat white teeth. Not only was he incredibly attractive, but he was enjoying Sarah teasing him. Damn, Sarah thought silently. I'll have to watch myself with this one. She was still toying with the idea of lassoing him, and possibly snogging his lips off before storing him away with the shirt boxes to enjoy again later.

"It's not that kind of Cruise," he said, leaning closer over the counter. Sarah felt her pulse quicken even more. She could hardly hear what he was saying for her own heart pounding in her ears now. Andy Ross and his orchestra were building up into a crescendo. They never sounded that good on the stage on a Saturday night. "The Chelsea cruise is not some kind of ocean going liner, it's a lot of classic cars and motorbikes that parade along Chelsea embankment for everyone to admire. If you fancy it, I'll take you to have a look. It's a lot of fun. People dress up too, you get the leather clad bikers, and the American fifties types like at the rock and roll dance.."

Before Sarah could open her mouth, Suzy butted in "Oooh, would you take me, too? I LOVE classic cars, especially those gorgeous old American ones, like..er..um… Cadillac's! You must have a mate who I could go with? I don't wanna play gooseberry of course! We could.. sort of..er..double date?" The girl had no shame, thought Sarah, and as far as she knew, Suzy would not know a classic car if it jumped up and bit her on the bum. Cadillac? where did she pull that one from? But James Dean was laughing now. Oh heavens, he was truly divine. Even his laugh was sexy. "Okay, if it makes your mate agree to go out with me, we can have a double date. I'll fix you up with my mate Billy. What do you say?"

Sarah was still trying to avoid eye contact. She knew if she looked into those devastatingly blue eyes one more time she would have agreed to try mud wrestling if he had asked her to. He really was drop-dead gob smackingly, amazingly heart juddering gorgeous. Mr Gorgeous gorge from gorgeous town. She had the urge to grab the big roll of silver paper and wrap him up in it, and take him home after work to savour and unwrap later. She would have agreed to go train spotting with this one, she suddenly realised. She was so pleased she had temporarily lost the power of speech, and stood there, gazing into those bluest of blue eyes that she was trying to avoid.

Sarah felt Suzy give her a sly nudge. She had obviously taken too long to reply. She had been too busy trying not to fall into those remarkable eyes of his. "Well, Okay, but you had better not turn up on some clapped out old moped, I'd die of shame" She said, eventually. She smiled at him as she spoke, just so he knew she was only kidding. Laughing, he told her he wouldn't let her down, then winked and added, "My names Jonny Mason, by the way. Very pleased to meet you"

They arranged to meet by the Angel Station On Saturday night at seven o'clock. Incredibly, he had said he lived in Duncan Terrace, which was just round the corner from the Angel Station, and just down the road from where Sarah and Suzy lived. On a pleasant summer evening, the two girls had often wandered home past Duncan Terrace, across ColeBrook Road and sauntered along by the canal. They called it their scenic route. Suzy was convinced he must have been making it up. They knew all the local boys in their area, surely one this good looking could not have slipped through her very stringent net. "How come we've never seen you around?" Suzy had blurted out, nosily, "You don't sound like you're a local boy!"

"That's because I'm not. My dad has just rented an antique shop in Camden Passage, we buy and sell antique toys, and so we moved to be near the business. We only moved in a month ago." Sarah and Suzy exchanged looks. Camden Passage was full of expensive antique shops, and Duncan Terrace had rows of gorgeous stylish houses, all overlooking a pretty little tree lined square. It was right by the Angel underground station. Sarah and Suzy passed it every morning on their way to work. You were talking serious money. Only the very wealthy could afford to live at the posh end of Islington. Sarah could tell that Suzy would be really impressed if Jonny's family were rich.

Suzy hoped that Jonny's mate would be loaded too. She couldn't wait for their double date.

Jonny didn't tell Sarah that he hadn't been able to believe his luck when he had spotted Sarah and Suzy at the bus stop at the Angel earlier that morning wearing their Debenhams uniforms. He had been crossing at the lights by the Angel station when he had seen them on the other side of the road. Sarah's beautiful long red hair had caught his eye. He had not been able to stop thinking about the beautiful red headed girl he had met at the Lyceum on Saturday. At first when he had spotted her, he thought he must have been hallucinating, or that it was wishful thinking. He had thought she had said she lived near the Angel when they had been on the dance floor. He had been looking for her amongst the busy high street ever since. He could not help himself. All week he had been up and down the high street, hoping that he might see her.

He was supposed to be on his way to an auction today, but he had left the house ridiculously early, during rush hour, hoping that he might catch a glimpse of the girl on the dance floor. He knew it was stupid, but he was obsessed. When he had spotted her, he could not quite believe it. He had forgotten all about the auction.

The showroom he was supposed to be heading for was in Essex Road, not far from the new shop in Camden Passage. His dad had spotted two Gottschalk dolls houses for sale in their catalogue, and had instructed Jonny to go and bid for them. The auction was not until eleven, but Jonny had thought he could get there early and have a good nose around first. It always paid to do a bit of research before an auction. You could find out who else was interested in things, and estimate who was prepared to pay top dollar. He had a few hours to kill though. The auction showroom did not open until 10.a.m. He had planned to grab a coffee and have a late breakfast in a café before going to look at the showroom. He had not planned on getting side tracked.

He had followed Sarah all the way to Oxford Street, Jumping on the 73 bus behind the one that the two girls had boarded. He had bought a cheap piece of junk just so he had an excuse to go and talk to her when he eventually spotted her behind the gift-wrapping counter. It had taken him nearly an hour to find which department she worked in, but his persistence had been worth it. It really was her, the girl from the Lyceum! He still could not quite believe his fortitude. He had been afraid he would never see her again, had already planned to go to as many events at the Lyceum in the future, just in case she was there too. He hoped he could maintain his casual "fancy seeing you here" face as he approached the girl of his dreams. He had forgotten all about the auction now. His dad would probably disinherit him for not bidding on the dolls houses, but Jonny was not too worried. All he was worried about now was his pounding heart, and making a good impression on his lovely red head.

Jonny had promised that he and his mate Billy would pick them up in something very special. Suzy was beside herself with excitement. "Oh gawd, I hope his mate is decent looking," she said to Sarah, as she put on lipstick in front of her dressing table mirror. She was getting ready for the much talked about double date.

Sarah had arrived twenty minutes ago. She was now sitting perched on the end of Suzy's bed, tapping her foot nervously. She had never felt nervous before a date before and did not like it. She wasn't ready to feel this way about a fella. She had toyed with the idea of not turning up, but she knew Suzy would kill her. She also knew that she really wanted to see Jonny. She hoped that her nerves would settle down, she felt sick now. Sick, but excited and happy all at the same time.

Suzy's bedroom looked like burglars had ransacked it. Clothes were strewn on every available surface, shoes were lying in a higgledy-piggledy pile beside the open wardrobe and the dressing table had make up, jewellery and nail varnish bottles spread out untidily on top. Suzy had tried on every outfit she possessed, and still was not happy with the outfit she had settled for. "Do I look alright?" she asked anxiously, for the fourth time. "You look fine!" Sarah said impatiently, "And do give over, you're making me even more nervous, now!"

Ten minutes later, Suzy was finally ready to leave. The pair of them had twirled and received approving looks from Suzy's mum and dad. The two girls walked along Goswell Road towards the Angel station. Suzy had finally settled on a pair of navy blue trousers and a pale blue blouse to wear. She was wearing navy blue and white platform soled shoes. She carried a matching blue and white clutch bag. She had a light blue cashmere cardigan slung casually around her shoulders. Suzy had bought it from Marks and Spencer during her lunch break. It had been hideously expensive, but she planned to return it on Monday and get a refund. Suzy often supplemented her wardrobe in this way, much to Sarah's amusement. Sarah had to admire her friend's cheek.

It was a pleasant warm evening, and Suzy was looking forward to seeing Jonny's friend. If he was only half as good looking as Jonny James Dean Mason, she told herself, she would still be a very happy girl.

Sarah had chosen a pale mint green dress to wear. She had only bought it a few days ago, and had not worn it yet. It was a very feminine dress. It had tiny pale pink flower sprigs on it, and wasn't the usual thing she would choose, but the style of it had reminded her of the dresses she had seen her mum wear in photo's back in the war years, and she thought Jonny might like it. It was classically stylish. She had never made such an effort for a boy before. She wasn't sure she liked it, she didn't ever want to get serious about a fella, but somehow, she had found herself caring about this one without her consent. She had teamed her dress with her favourite shoes, tee bar high heels, in pale pink, and she had a matching pale pink handbag to complete her outfit. In case she got chilly she had brought a light jacket, but was carrying it now, folded over her arm.

They were late. It was ten past seven when they saw the Angel station in front of them. Sarah spotted Jonny already waiting outside. He looked a bit anxious, but his face lit up when he spotted the two girls approaching. He was standing next to a tall black haired fella, and they had both spotted them now. Jonny smiled, and waved. The tall black haired fella was not giving anything away. Sarah didn't want to admit that her heart had turned over at the sight of Jonny. Even from a distance, he still looked good enough to eat.

Carrie Miller struggled to sit up. Her ribs ached, and her lip was sore and throbbing. Her white blouse was ruined as it was covered in her own blood. The room began to spin as she sat, and she felt sick, so she tried her best to keep very still until the dizziness and queasiness passed. Slowly, she pulled herself up and went to check herself in the bathroom mirror. This time, he had split her lip and made her nose bleed, and she knew from experience that he had bruised or cracked her ribs again. She should really get herself to the hospital but it was Saturday night, and she could not face another night sitting aching for hours with all the other sad cases, and see the knowing looks of the nurses and doctors. Over the years, she had become a regular in the casualty department. She told herself grimly that she should have a reserved sign to put on one of the waiting room chairs. The doctors, many of whom she recognised now, looked at her with pity in their eyes, and had urged her repeatedly to prosecute. It was embarrassing, and Carrie was ashamed that she did not have the courage to follow their advice. Instead, she cleaned herself up as best she could, made herself a cuppa and crawled into bed.

Tommy had slammed out of the house, and she knew he would not be home until the works social club had shut. Hopefully he would be blind drunk as usual, and collapse in a heap on the sofa as he normally did. Thankfully, Sarah was out having a good time and would not see her mum in such a state. She hoped Sarah would never find out that the row this time was about Sarah going out on a date. Tommy had said that Carrie should not encourage her to go out with boys. He knew what they were like; they were only after one thing. Carrie had said that Sarah was young, it was good for her to go out and have a good time, and Tommy had said he did not want his daughter to be a good time girl, turning into a little slag wearing too much make up and sleeping with any bloke that gave her the eye. Carrie had automatically leapt to Sarah's defence, and realised too late that Tommy always had to be in the right. She wanted to bite her tongue and reel her words back in, but of course, it was way too late for that.

It had descended very quickly into a row, as it invariably did these days, and even though Carrie had shut up very quickly, trying desperately to nip Tommy's anger in the bud, it had gone too far. Once Tommy had the bit between his teeth, he would not stop until he lashed out.

Carrie knew that Sarah would notice her fat lip, Sarah never missed a trick, but Carrie was too bruised to worry about that right now. She swallowed a couple of pain killers, which was difficult with her lip, then she lay down carefully on the bed, mindful of her ribs, and tried her best to get some sleep while the flat was peaceful. She let her tea go cold as she lay crying silently into the darkness.

The Chelsea Cruise had been a fabulous idea. Sarah had really enjoyed herself. Jonny had been a perfect gent, and charming company. She felt elated, the way she always imagined it would feel if she was on drugs. She could feel her cheeks glowing with excitement. All her nerves had quickly evaporated and she found herself having the time of her life. She had promised herself that she would remain aloof, and not fall into those blue eyes of Jonny but all her plans had failed miserably. She tried, she really did, but Jonny was impossible to resist. She found herself having such a good time that she no longer cared about her own mantra, the one where if you cared they would hurt you, just because they could. Jonny was definitely addictive, and she was powerless to resist.

The Chelsea embankment was obviously, where all the beautiful people went to hang out, and all the cars really were spectacular. Jonny looked as if he belonged there. The river

Thames looked magical in the moonlight, with fairy lights strung all along the embankment, twinkling prettily and reflected in the water. Jonny had told Sarah the make of each car as it passed, but Sarah could not remember them. She did not have any interest in cars really, but Jonny's enthusiasm was infectious and she had to admit that some of the vintage ones were incredibly impressive. Jonny had laughed and his beautiful blue eyes had twinkled when she said, "Ooh, I like that shiny red one!" and he had hugged her and told her it had been a T Bird or something, but she had winked wickedly and said, "Yes, that's what I said, a red one"

Jonny and Billy were a good double act, and kept the delighted girls entertained all evening. Billy Jameson, Suzy had been delighted to see, was a decent looking lad. He was twenty-two, like Jonny, had a cheeky grin and even cheekier brown eyes. He was more than a match for Suzy, and the banter between the four of them had kept going all night. As the evening wore on, Sarah thought that Billy was a little bit flash; he did not have the same genuine warmth about him that Jonny had, but she was having such a good time with Jonny that she decided to be charitable. Maybe she would warm to him a bit more as time went on.

Suzy had been slightly disappointed when Billy had spoken for the first time, and she realised he had an even broader cockney accent than her own, and her heart had sunk to her shoes when he let slip he lived on the Packington Estate, that was just off of Essex Road. The Packington Estate was notorious in Islington, and it had a reputation for breeding hard nuts that got in to, or caused trouble. However, This Billy was drop dead sexy, and Suzy had decided to give him a chance. She did not want to seem like a snob. Besides, he had been an amazing kisser.

Jonny had actually whistled in appreciation at the start of the evening, as the two girls walked up to them by the station. He could not stop himself. Sarah looked absolutely stunning. Sarah had felt herself blush, but was secretly pleased. She liked the way he wore his heart on his sleeve yet still appeared amazingly cool at the same time. "You look sensational!" he had said, grinning appreciatively from ear to ear. "Come on, the car is parked round the corner."

Sarah and Suzy had not been able to get over the car. It was a highly polished racing green E type Jag. Sarah had not been expecting anything quite so swanky. It was very posh and had beige leather seats and a walnut dashboard. Jonny was very keen to show it off. It was immaculate. Even the wheels were sparkling, and Sarah could see her reflection in the shiny paintwork. Jonny was visibly pleased at the girl's faces. "You didn't nick it, did you?" Sarah blurted out without thinking. Jonny roared with laughter. "Don't be daft!" He said. He told her as he unlocked the door that he had always loved classic cars, and this one just happened to belong to his father. Billy was busy telling Suzy that he worked in the garage in Highbury where Jonny's dad took his pride and joy for a service. That was where Jonny and Billy had met. They had got talking about cars a few years ago and got on like a house on fire. As Jonny was new to the area, Billy had he said, offered to show him around.

"I'd better look after it," Jonny had said with a grin, as he held the door open carefully for the girls to get in, "If anything happens to his pride and joy, I'm history"

"Er...does he know you've got it tonight?" Sarah had said, nervously.

"Well, hopefully, he won't ever find out" Jonny said, grinning mischievously. Actually, Jonny adored his father and would not have dreamt of taking his father's beloved car without his knowledge. A bit of teasing was too much fun to resist though. Sarah looked panic stricken, but the others just laughed, so she thought, oh, blow it, it's not my problem, and climbed inside.

It was a long way to Chelsea, and she rested her head back on the smooth leather seat, and prepared to enjoy the ride. She had never been in a car this luxurious before, and had definitely never been out with such a lovely fella before. She felt a tingle of excitement run through her veins as Jonny started the engine and it roared into life.

Jonny had driven the girl's home at the end of the evening, and had pulled up in Sebastian Street to let them out. Billy and Suzy were having a kiss and a cuddle on the back seat. Jonny gazed into Sarah's big grey eyes and gave her a soft, sweet little kiss. She was suddenly bashful and did not want to have a full-blown snog in front of Suzy and Billy it seemed cheap. She was grateful that Jonny seemed to feel the same way. She could not remember ever feeling happier than she did right now, sitting beside this gorgeous chap. Happy, but afraid at the same time. If she let her guard down, she knew she would be vulnerable, and she did not like that idea one little bit. She had already been much keener this evening than she had intended to be. They arranged to go on another date next weekend and despite her fear, Sarah was delighted when Jonny asked for her phone number, and promised to ring her in the week.

After the boys roared off in the jag, the girls stood for a while on the street corner, dissecting the evening excitedly. "Oooh, he's a really good snog!" Suzy said dreamily, "I wonder what he's like in the sack?"

"Suzy!" Sarah said, looking shocked, "You've only known him five minutes! Give yourself a bit of time to get to know him first before you rip his trousers off!"

Suzy waved her hand in the air as if she was swatting a fly, and then exclaimed, "Why the bloody hell should I hang about? I'm on the pill, so what's the point hanging around? I'm young, randy and need a bit of fun in my life. I reckon Billy boy thinks the same way. You're far too straight laced missy, that's your problem. You should let your hair down occasionally! A good shag would do you the power of good!" She nudged her friend affectionately to take the sting out of her words.

"I'm waiting for the right bloke to come along" Sarah said defensively. "I couldn't ever.. well, you know, just do it with someone I hardly know."

"Rubbish! You just haven't met anyone yet who you fancy enough. What about Jonny, though? Blimey, if he doesn't float your boat, there must be something wrong with you. Go on, admit it, you want to rip his Y fronts off and roger him rigid, don't you?" Sarah went a delicate shade of beetroot red., but giggled.

"Shut your face!" she said, once she had regained the power of speech. The girl's laughter peeled out into the cool night air.

  Eventually, Sarah said she had better go, and both girls floated off happily, each wrapped in their own happy thoughts.

Sarah came down to earth with a hefty bump as soon as she put her key in the lock and opened the front door. She heard her dad snoring loudly, and knew he would be in a drunken stupor on their brown dralon couch even before the stench of stale booze and fags assaulted her nostrils. She peered gingerly round the front room door, and there he was, flat out, mouth open, beer belly heaving up and down, snoring like a wart hog. He sickened her. Once upon a time, he must have been a handsome man. Her mum still kept a wedding photo of the pair of them on the mantelpiece above their little three bar gas fire. Sarah looked over at it. She could see it from the light in the hall passage. Her mum always left the hall light on for her bless her. She said she did not want Sarah coming into a dark flat after a night out.

 Her mum looked beautiful and really happy in the black and white photograph on the mantelpiece. She was standing, smiling in her two-piece suit, or costume, as her mum always called it, and her dad looked smart and yes, he was handsome. They were both so young, and looked very much in love. Sarah wondered how on earth it had come to this. She thought, in a panic, what would her life be like in twenty years, would a bloke like Jonny turn out to be a wife beater? It made her feel sick. She heard her dad grunt in his sleep, and she jumped out of her skin. She did not want to wake him up, so she crept out of the living room and went to get herself ready for bed.

Sunday morning arrived, and Sarah had slept late. She lay in her bed, drowsily reliving every moment of the lovely time she had had the night before. She could still feel the soft sweet little kiss Jonny had given her, and smiled at the memory of his sapphire blue eyes and lovely long eyelashes. She heard her mum knock softly on her door and say quietly "Sarah, love, are you awake? I've made you a cup of tea"

"Yeah, thanks. Come in mum"

The door opened, and her mum came in with her tea. As soon as Sarah sat up, she saw her mums face, and noticed the fat lip. Judging by the way that her mum winced when she reached to put the cup down, Sarah guessed she had bruises elsewhere too. Sarah sighed. Not again! "Mum, what happened this time?"

It was Monday morning and Tommy Miller was glad to be on his way to work. He was worried about Spartacus, his favourite horse. He had not been his usual placid gentle self on Friday, and he hoped that Will the stable lad had kept him warm over the weekend. Tommy had had this weekend off, though he wished he had not. All he had done was row with the wife, and even his Sarah was growing up to be a right little bitch, just like her mother. These days Sarah never knew when to keep her gob shut, and he was beginning to think it was high time he gave her a good hiding, so she knew her place. Mind you, he told himself, a good hiding hadn't taught the wife to mind her manners. She still knew how to rattle his cage, and never learned her lesson. He knew he had a short temper, but my God, she really knew how to rub him up the wrong way.

Things had become worse lately he had to admit. It was all Carrie's fault though. He couldn't help it. He told himself that he had diabetes, and the high blood sugar made him short tempered. He knew deep down that he was just making excuses, but it helped him to feel less guilty if he told himself it was not his fault, he could not help himself. His condition made him so angry. He liked feeling sorry for himself. He told Carrie that she didn't know what it was like. She didn't have to inject herself with insulin four times every day. She didn't get hypo's if her blood glucose levels fell too low or hyper's if her blood glucose climbed too high, and have to watch what she ate all the time in order to try and keep her blood sugar stable. He had to test his own blood throughout the day to check his glucose levels. He was like a ruddy pincushion. He knew he was being unfair, that his temper had been violent long before the diabetes had developed, and he also knew that he smoked and drank far too much and was a nasty mean drunk, but he conveniently chose to forget that. He had put on a lot of weight over the years too, and had a large beer belly, which definitely did not help his condition, but he was tired of the doctors lecturing him all the bloody time. He was entitled to a bit of enjoyment at his time of life, surely, and he liked a pint.

 His doctor told him off for smoking, and for liking a bacon sarnie and a bit of chocolate. If he couldn't enjoy a treat now and then, he grumbled to himself, then what was the fucking point of it all? He crossed over at City Road, throwing the stub of his roll up into the curb and headed along Shepherdess walk towards the stables.

Sarah had not wanted to leave her mum, and had told her she would ring in sick, but Carrie had insisted that she go to work, not wanting her to get into trouble. Sarah had reluctantly agreed to go, but had made her mum promise to go to the doctor, and get herself looked at. She suspected that mum had broken ribs. She was covered in bruises. "You should call the police, and get the bastard put away!" Sarah said vehemently, as she helped her mum get dressed. Carrie sat on the edge of the bed, holding her side, and Sarah was gently trying to help her mum put on a blouse. "Sarah!" her mum said, actually sounding shocked, "Stop that swearing! He's your father!"

"Yes he is, to my dying shame! Why the hell do you still stick up for him? Don't you dare defend him, Mum, whatever he did or didn't do in the bloody war is no excuse! He's a bloody animal!"

Carrie felt the colour rising in her face. She was so ashamed. She knew her daughter was right, but over the year's she had become nothing more than a shadow, a pathetic victim, and she hated herself for it. She lived every day in fear, jumping when she heard his key turn in the lock, trying to placate him, trying to read his mood, to avoid upsetting him, to remember the happy days when they had been courting. She tried to keep the peace for Sarah's sake, and it had become such a habit, she didn't know how to stop it. She was afraid to stay, but so much more afraid of being alone. What would she do? Where could she go? She had very little money, she still did her cleaning job, but it didn't pay very much. She didn't have the confidence now to find anything better. With no money, no family, other than Sarah, how could she possibly support herself? She wouldn't dream of going to one of those women's shelters. She had been given a leaflet once at the casualty department. It had a number to call, but she had thrown it away.

She didn't want anyone to know, it was too shameful. She would manage; she had had years of practise. She was trapped and she knew it. All the sparkle and spirit she had once had as a young girl that had ironically, attracted Tommy to her in the first place, had been knocked out of her. A tear fell on to her cheek. Sarah knelt down in front of her mother. "Oh Mum!" she said sadly, and hugged her, then apologised as she realised it hurt, "Mum, we can't go on like this, it's not right. If he does this again, I swear, I'll bloody kill him!"

It had been a long day, and Tommy Miller was just finishing up at the stables. Spartacus seemed much better, and although he had not been pulling his wagon today, Tommy had stopped by his stable to say hello to him, and give him a good night pat. As he turned to leave, he dropped his cap, and without thinking, bent down to pick it up.

He had broken the golden rule about bending down behind a horse. It cost him dearly. He did not see the wasp that stung his favourite horse, but he heard the loud frightened whinny a split second before he felt the kick to his head that knocked him out cold, and fractured his skull.

CHAPTER THREE

All the time her father was in the hospital, Sarah hoped that he would not recover. She refused to feel guilty about wishing her father dead. The way he was, he would be better off, anyway. That horse had done an awful lot of damage. Secretly, she was very grateful to that horse. Her dad's skull had been fractured and he had suffered a blood clot on the brain. He had regained consciousness in hospital the day after emergency surgery, but the blood clot had caused him to have a stroke. He was conscious, but unable to move his left arm or leg, or talk. His face had drooped, and his mouth hung down in a hideous grimace. The doctors had said he might never fully recover.

Carrie had been visiting every day, but Sarah had only been to see him a few times. She could not bear to look at him; it was too cruel, even for her father. Hospitals made her feel uncomfortable. She hated the depressing green walls and smell of disinfectant. The smell evoked ugly memories of sitting for hours in waiting rooms over the years while her poor battered mother had been patched up yet again. Life would be so much easier if her dad never left hospital. As much as she hated him for all the beatings he had given her mum over the years, she had not wanted him to end up like this. She had always hoped her mother would find the courage to leave him, but she would not wish this fate on anyone, not even her vicious father. Life really wasn't fair sometimes, Sarah thought, grimly.

A young nurse pulled the curtains around her father's bed in order to clean him, and Sarah had to go. It was all so undignified, she could not bear it a second longer. She longed to see Jonny and escape the hospital ward. Jonny had been incredibly supportive when Sarah had told him about her father's accident. He was so close to his own father he had assumed that Sarah would be devastated. He had been quite taken aback when she had said that her father was better off out of the way. Sarah had tried to stay nonchalant when she spoke about her father's temper and his unending cruelty to her mother, but despite herself, her voice had become thick with emotion. Jonny, appalled that any man could inflict such misery on a woman, and annoyed at his own naivety for not even realising such violence went on behind closed doors, had felt out of his depth. He had only been able to hold his beautiful Sarah close to him, and tell her that he would always be there to listen and help in any way he could.

With her dad safely tucked up in a hospital ward, however, Sarah had been astonished because she had seen her mum blossom as never before. At first, Carrie had seemed a bit lost, and wondered around the flat still cowed, as if Tommy might appear and fly into a rage at any moment. However, as the days turned into weeks, and then months, Sarah saw a change in her mother. Without the worry of dear old dad, and his constant ominous presence and wandering fists, her mum looked at least ten years younger. Sarah saw her mum looking relaxed and happy. The two women had been able to watch whatever they liked on telly, laugh and joke, and listen to music together. It had been blissful.

As the weeks passed, Sarah and Carrie had eaten their evening meals together, Sarah told her mum about her day at work, and home life for the first time was happy and relaxed. Sarah had never seen her mother like that before. She was a different person light hearted and carefree. It was lovely to hear her mum sing along with the wireless every morning, and not have to see her beautiful face pinched and worried all the time, or looking anxiously at the clock when it got near the time Tommy would be home from work. Carrie had even agreed to go to play bingo once a week with Suzy's mum Joycie. She was tasting a bit of independence, and loving every minute of it. Carrie even wondered whether she dared look for another job, one that would pay a bit more, and give her a bit more scope.

Sarah had been on regular dates with Jonny, and had enjoyed every moment of their time together. He had, so far proved himself trustworthy. Sarah had been impressed when he had rung her as promised after the first date, and they had chatted excitedly and easily together for ages. She had been so impressed at the support he had given her when she had reluctantly told him about her dad being in hospital. Sarah had even brought him home to meet her mum. Without her dad around, it had seemed a natural thing to do. He had turned up cheerfully, with a big box of chocolates for her mum, and a huge bouquet of pink roses for her. He had chatted easily with Carrie, and had made a real effort. Her mum had been bowled over, and told her after he left that he was a lovely young man, and added that she should hang on to this one. Sarah was delighted that her mum had approved, because, despite herself, she knew that she had fallen for Jonny Mason.

Sarah lay in bed after turning off her bedside lamp and snuggled down under the covers. Jonny had gone home after dropping her off safely from the pictures. They had had another lovely evening together. He made her laugh, his kisses thrilled her, and he had always rung when he said he would. Sarah felt her heart and her pulse quicken just thinking about him. She lay and relived every moment of their evening together as she snuggled down all cosy and warm under the covers. She could hear her mum chuckling in the living room. She was still up watching the telly. It was so good to hear her laugh. Sarah closed her eyes, let her mind drift and began to reminisce about the happy days she had shared with her mum as a child, before she was old enough to realise exactly what was going on at home. She wondered if maybe her dad was not as bad back then. It all seemed so far off, it was difficult to pinpoint in her mind the first time she had become aware of the violence that lurked inside her father.

As a child, her dad had just been a distant figure who was out at work a lot, and Sarah soon learned to stay out of his way and be quiet when he was at home. Her mother had laughed a lot back then. She had always been close to her mother, maybe because she was an only child, but her mum was always patient and kind to her, and always around. Sarah had loved going on shopping trips with her mum. She had fond memories of walking to Exmouth Street market, holding her mums hand, and waiting patiently as mummy went in to the butchers, then along to the bakers to buy a nice crusty loaf of fresh bread and maybe some buns for tea. Then they would cross the road to the Home and Colonial grocery shop. She had loved to watch the sales assistants in their clean white aprons, slice up the bacon or ham, or veal and ham pie.

The Home and Colonial had pretty tiled walls and many glass counters with mouth-watering meats and cheeses on display. Sometimes as a special treat, mummy would take her in to the pie and mash shop. They would sit on the wooden benches at the marble-topped tables, eat their pie mash, and liquor all covered in vinegar, with spoons and forks before continuing their shopping.

After lunch mum would walk a bit further and they would have a look in Woolworths. Sarah loved the pick and mix counters, and the open glass topped displays. Mum would let Sarah help to choose the broken biscuits that were displayed like the pick and mix. Mum would hand the big paper bag to the sales girl, and she would check the weight and twist the bag over to seal it. Sometimes, if Sarah were a good girl, Mum would buy her a scrapbook. When they got home from shopping, mum would mix up some flour and water paste, and give Sarah her old Kensita coupon catalogues. Sarah would sit happily for hours, cutting out her favourite pictures and sticking them into her scrapbook. Sarah remembered her mum counting out the coupons from her Kensitas cigarettes. Sarah would be at one end of the kitchen table with her scrapbook and mum would be busy counting at the other.

Mum would let Sarah look in the Kensitas catalogue, and sometimes choose a toy she liked. When Carrie had enough coupons, she would put them all into her big blue and white shopping bag, and Carrie and Sarah would walk to the Kensitas showroom in Old Street. The ladies in the showroom would weigh out the coupons to check that there was the correct amount, and then hand over whatever you had ordered. Carrie had managed to stop smoking now, and Sarah was glad, as she had always hated the smell but she did have fond memories of the presents bought from that show room. She had a little dog on wheels as a toddler, with a long handle to help her learn how to walk, and a big cuddly bunny rabbit with lovely soft ears when she started school. Sarah wondered sleepily whatever had happened to those much-loved toys as she drifted off to sleep.

When Sarah was small, her mother had a part time job working in the little launderette that was on their council estate. Carrie had worked there for a long time. She would walk through the playground of the flats every day wearing her floral nylon overall that protected her clothes. During the war, Carrie had given up working in the cigarette factory down the road to work in a munitions factory. She had trained as a precision engineer and was highly skilled with machinery. She knew exactly how those washing machines worked in the launderette and how to get them to work without putting in any money. Mum had what she called her "tickling stick" and she would use the stick almost like a magic wand, inserting it in a strategic place to make the machine run. She could then pocket the money from the service washes for herself. She was very careful not to get too greedy. Every day at 4p.m her boss, Mrs Mathias, would come into the launderette wearing a fur hat, a matching fur trimmed coat and white cotton gloves to empty the machines and count the days takings. If one machine had noticeably less money in it than any of the others, she would get suspicious, and she would certainly notice if the day's takings were lighter than usual. Sarah's mum did not see what she did as stealing. She saw it as survival. Tommy did not give her enough housekeeping to live on, and the wages Mrs Mathias paid her were meagre. She was not even allowed to accept the tips that grateful customers often gave her. She had to put them all in a jar, and Mrs Mathias made sure all tips went straight in to her own purse.

That, Carrie thought, was incredibly mean and unfair so Carrie Miller did what she had to do. Sarah, lying in bed with her eyes closed, smiled at the memory. Even though she was only a little girl, she had understood what her mum was up to, and was very careful to keep her mums secret safe. Her mum laughed, because Sarah could never pronounce "Mrs Mathias" and always called her "Mrs Mafia"

Mrs Mafia became suspicious about Carrie after a tip off from a regular customer. Sometimes Carrie would feel sorry for a particular customer, if she thought they were down on their luck, and let them use one of the machines free of charge. Other customers got jealous, and grumbled that they thought they deserved preferential treatment, too. It was only a matter of time before a nosy parker let the cat out of the bag. Mrs Mafia had no proof, so she told Carrie that if she went quietly she would not prosecute her for stealing. Carrie really had no choice but to leave. She had been furious when she discovered that the nosy parker who had grassed her up was her new replacement as launderette manager.

Carrie had been lucky and found another job straight away, however. It was making tea and cleaning in a sewing factory in St John Street. She had known that she would get a good hiding from Tommy if he had discovered she had got herself sacked from the launderette. She had told him that the new job paid more money, and he had been quite happy about that. It was a lie, of course, but Carrie did what she had to do to survive once again.

Carrie had liked the new job. There was no one breathing down her neck as she worked. The machinists in the sewing factory were a nice bunch, and if she ever had to take Sarah with her, they would make a fuss of her, and even ran up some soft toys for her from off cuts of spare material. Sarah still had the rag doll one of the lovely ladies had sewn for her. She still sat on Sarah's bedroom chair. A little faded now, but still smiling the same sweet hand stitched smile. She had called the dolly Rosie, as the lady had made her a dress that had pink roses on it, and she had rosy red felt cheeks.

Carrie would save her wages to treat Sarah, and on Friday's after school Carrie would take her little girls hand and together they would walk to Solly's, the most magical place on earth, the toy shop in Exmouth Street market. Sarah loved Mr Solly. He was a small, dapper little man, with thinning black hair and round horn rimmed spectacles. He always had a welcoming smile on his face for all his child customers, and would invite Sarah into the shop with a cheery "Hello my dear Miss Sarah! I am delighted to see you again! Do come in, and feel free to browse"

He would ask Sarah how much she had to spend today, and Sarah would shyly hold out her hand with her coins for Mr Solly to see. Then he would patiently show Sarah where to look, and what she could afford.

Oh, the treasures that her eyes beheld on those magnificent shelves! Mum and Mr Solly would wait patiently while Sarah considered her precious purchase, and looked longingly at all of the other delights that she hoped to be able to afford one day. Sarah had given away most of her toys and games when she became too old for them, but some of her treasures bought from Mr Solly were still at the back of her wardrobe. She knew she would never part with them; they had too much sentimental value. She had kept a little plastic toy fridge, still complete with its little plastic bottles of milk and pretend storage containers. She had played with that for so many happy hours, pretending to take food out and cooking it for all her dollies. She still had her Sindy dolls, of course, and a shoebox full of outfits for them. She probably still had her medallion from the Sindy club somewhere. She and Suzy had both been members. Drowsily, Sarah yawned, and drifted into a peaceful sleep. It was so good to be safe in her cosy bed without the sound of her dad's voice raised in anger, and without the worry of what he might do to her mother in the next room. Knowing that her father was not coming home any time soon to spoil things, Sarah slept peacefully every night and woke up to the sound of her mum singing in the kitchen.

Sarah was nervous, as Jonny had invited her to his house. They had been dating for three months now, and Jonny said it was high time he introduced her to his dad. Jonny said he wanted to show her off to all his friends and family. That had made Sarah even more nervous. "Oh, no pressure then!" she had said to a grinning Jonny. "Don't be daft!" Jonny said, kissing the tip of her nose and giving her a squeeze. "There's no need to be nervous. My dad's great, just be yourself. We'll have a great time. It's dad's birthday and we're having a party for him"

Jonny lived with his father. He had told Sarah that his mum had died of breast cancer when he was just two years old. Sarah loved the way Jonny became animated and his face lit up when he spoke about his father. She envied him. They obviously adored one another. Jonny's dad had let Jonny have the upper part of the new house, and he had had it converted into a self-contained flat just for him. Sarah was very impressed, and dying to see it. Jonny told her that he was thrilled to have a place of his own, and he had decorated it himself and helped to fit the kitchen. He had been asking Sarah to come round and see his flat for ages, but Sarah had so far resisted. She was nervous about it she had to admit. She did not think she would be able to resist Jonny if she was alone with him in his flat. Sarah had got all bashful because when Jonny had said that he had not only helped to fit the kitchen and decorate the flat but he could cook as well she had stupidly remarked that she liked a fella to be good with his hands. Jonny had winked at her wickedly and replied that he would do his best to oblige. Jonny loved the way she got bashful, and he teased her about it often. Sarah did not really mind. She didn't think she could resist the delectable Jonny for much longer.

Sarah was looking forward to meeting Jonny's father despite her nerves. He was having a party for his birthday, but had told Jonny to invite all his friends, the more the merrier. Sarah could tell that Jonny absolutely hero-worshipped his father, and the way he described him, it was no wonder, he sounded like a wonderful man.

He had brought Jonny up single handed and had showered him with love all his life. She only hoped that he and Jonny's friends would approve of her. Jonny had been surprised at the way Sarah spoke of her own father. When Sarah had said he was in hospital he had volunteered to go with her to visit him and Sarah had been quite horrified at the very idea. She had finally confided in Jonny and told him that her father was not a very nice man. She could tell that Jonny was shocked, but he had said no more. He had merely held her close to him, offered his support if she needed it and kissed her tenderly.

Suzy and Billy had been invited to the party too, and Jonny had told her a few of his old mates from school that he still kept in touch with would be going, as well as all his father's friends and a few relations. Sarah was looking forward to meeting everybody but was worried about making a good impression. She had agonised for ages on what outfit to wear for the occasion.

Suzy was sitting on Sarah's bed, impatiently waiting for Sarah to finish doing her hair. Suzy was dying to see inside Jonny's house, too. She was a nosy old bat, Sarah thought impatiently, as she fiddled with her hair dryer. Oh lor, why was it whenever she wanted to make a good impression, her hair would never go right? "Come on, give it ere!" Suzy said in exasperation, as Sarah looked panic stricken in the dressing table mirror at the state of her hair. "At this rate the party'll be over by the time we get there!" she took the dryer right out of Sarah's hands and blasted it at full throttle at her scalp. Sarah knew better than to object. She meekly handed over her styling brush, and allowed Suzy to do her worst with the dryer and the hairspray. Actually, Suzy was a pretty dab hand when it came to hairdressing. It did not take her long to dry Sarah's long silky mane, and help her choose an outfit. "Are you sure this dress is okay?" Sarah said doubtfully, after carefully stepping into it so as not to mess up her hair and makeup. She stood looking at herself dubiously in her full-length wardrobe mirror.

"For the last time, you look fucking gorgeous! Can we go now?"

Jonny opened the door, and his face lit up when he saw it was Sarah. Suzy did not think he had even noticed she was standing next to Sarah. She could not help feeling a bit envious. Jonny lived in a big posh house, had a rich dad, was bloody drop dead sexy and treated Sarah like a princess. Jonny was so obviously madly in love with Sarah. Suzy wished that Billy would look at her like that, but he never did. She had been a bit worried that Billy was getting bored with her. He had not said so, but he had definitely cooled towards her in the last few weeks. Besides, Billy still lived at home with his mum and dad and had to share a bedroom with his younger brother, Graham. He lived on a manky old council Estate, a notoriously rough council estate at that, just off Essex road. It was only a short walk away from where Jonny lived, but a different world from Jonny.

Suzy could not quite understand how Billy and Jonny had become friends in the first place, as they had nothing in common, other than a mutual love of cars. Suzy was beginning to feel a little uneasy around Billy. He had taken her to his home only once, and his mum had not exactly been welcoming.

His dad had said a curt hello in between puffing on a woodbine and his mum had looked her up and down as if she was sizing up a side of beef on a butchers slab. Suzy had felt really uncomfortable and did not want to set foot in there again. She had noticed that Billy behaved like a totally different person when Jonny was not around. He was all sweetness and light in front of Jonny, always had all the answers and agreed with everything that Jonny said. He came across as an articulate and witty person. The kind of person that Jonny approved of. When Billy was alone with Suzy, however, he was uncouth and starting to show his true colours. Suzy was beginning to think it was time to give Billy boy the old heave ho. He was a good kisser, but there were plenty of fish in the sea. Maybe it was time to throw this one back she mused, and try to land something better. He might be becoming bored with her, but she realised she did not really care. She decided that she was definitely growing tired of him.

Jonny welcomed them in, and took Sarah to the kitchen. Billy had appeared, and had taken Suzy off to get a drink. She had brought two bottles of wine, and Billy led her off in search of a corkscrew. Sarah sheepishly handed Jonny a card and a bottle of whisky for Jonny's dad and a biscuit tin she was carrying. "My mum insisted I bring this. It's filled with her homemade sausage rolls. She said it was bad manners to go to a party and not take something." She smiled shyly. Bless her, thought Jonny, fondly. He liked Sarah's mum. She was a top lady. His dad had hired caterers and the kitchen was positively groaning with food, but he took the tin Sarah proffered enthusiastically. "Ooh, homemade stuff, fantastic! The stuff in the kitchen all looks a bit poncy if you ask me! Tell your mum thanks, she is so lovely to go to so much trouble, and bless you for getting my dad his favourite whisky. I know he'll love it. I'll introduce you in a minute. Don't look so nervous, he's going to love you, just wait and see. Come on, let's go and put these on a plate."

He opened the lid as Sarah followed him to the kitchen, and took out two sausage rolls. They really did look and smell delicious. He took a big bite out of one. They really were very good, and he ate it greedily and began to nibble the next one. He made appreciative noises at Sarah, with his mouth still full, and with crumbs on his chin. Sarah grinned in relief, and laughed. She hadn't been sure if he would be embarrassed at the home made offerings. "Think I'll pinch a few more before the guests spot these" he said, with his mouth still full, "They're too good for this lot" Sarah hit him playfully and called him a greedy-guts. As Jonny went to a cupboard to get a plate, Sarah overheard a dark haired girl talking to her friend.

"Oh my God!" the loud braying voice screeched," Look at poor Jonny! Someone has actually brought something in a tatty old biscuit tin!" They both brayed then, like two horses in a stable waiting for their nosebags. Sarah felt herself blushing to the tips of her toes. She took a sneaky look to see who was speaking. Oh great! it was the irritating young girl who had kissed Jonny at the rock and roll revival dance at the Lyceum. Louise double barrelled name. Her friend really did have a long horse face and was now snorting, in what Sarah supposed was a rich bitch public school sort of way. They really did look the sort who spent a lot of time in stables, probably getting ready to go off round the countryside terrorising foxes, Sarah thought viciously.

Jonny had said that Louise whatsit had gone to a posh private school. She definitely looked the type, Sarah thought venomously. All money and no manners. The two spoilt girls were watching Jonny closely. He had not noticed, as he was busy arranging the sausage rolls on a plate. "Oh no! they're sausage rolls! Very working class! Jonny and his dad are getting down with the locals I see!" more laughter. They obviously thought sausage rolls were too down market for Jonny. Sarah had a sneaking suspicion that they knew she had brought them, and that they wanted her to overhear their conversation.

"Oh, please, they'll be getting out the cheese and pineapple next, and spearing them on cocktail sticks!" they both hooted with laughter at that, delighted at their own wit. "Oh yes, and then they'll cover half a grapefruit in tinfoil, and make a cheese and pineapple hedgehog!" this, apparently was too much for snotty and horse face, and they cackled even louder. Sarah stood and seethed, but then she saw the hideous Louise look straight at her and stage whisper "I bet his vulgar little shop girl girlfriend brought them"

Sarah was really hurt, and furious. She was itching to rip the vile girl's hair out, but she tried to hide it, as Jonny had finished arranging the sausage rolls, and said he would give her the grand tour of the house. He carefully carried a plate piled high with food, which included several of the sausage rolls he had carefully arranged on the serving plate, as he guided Sarah through the throng of people. She felt snotty and horse face giving her daggers as Jonny took her hand and led her through to the lavish living room. As they passed Louise and horse face,

Sarah smiled her nicest smile at Louise. She could feel the venom boring into her receding back as Jonny led her through the crowded room. Sarah hoped that seeing her and Jonny look so happy together would kill her with jealousy, and save her the trouble of having to throttle her herself.Jonny told Sarah peevishly that his dad had not been too happy when Louise had turned up with her friend, and said her father sent his apologies but couldn't make it. Louise had not even been invited, never mind her horsy pal. Victor had just been too polite to tell her.

They passed a very elegant blonde woman, who smiled at the pair of them. Jonny introduced Sarah to Marlayna Rudzinska, an old friend of his fathers. "Oi, not so much of the old!" the blonde woman said, smiling. She had a very attractive accent. "I am delighted to meet you, Sarah. " As she spoke, she stole one of Jonny's sausage rolls right off his plate, and winked. "These look too tasty to resist" she said, popping the pastry into her mouth. Sarah could not help laughing. Thank God, there was someone normal and friendly. Marlayna, swallowing and trying delicately to remove the crumbs from around her mouth, said to Jonny, "You had better make sure you save a few more of these for me"

Marlayna Rudzinska had been in love with Victor Mason for over fifteen years. It was the tragedy of her life that unfortunately Victor did not feel the same way. Indeed, he seemed to have absolutely no idea that Marlayna had any romantic feelings towards him whatsoever, but then, men could be remarkably thick sometimes, Marlayna thought sadly.

Marlayna had met Victor one cold winter day when they had been given stalls next to each other at an antique fair in York. Victor had been the perfect gent, and had shared his flask of lovely piping hot soup when he spotted how cold Marlayna looked. They had chatted for the rest of the day, and Marlayna was smitten. She had laughingly told him that she should be used to the cold as she was originally from Poland, but had obviously gone soft since moving to England. Over the coming years, their paths often crossed at antique fairs up and down the country, and a friendship was forged. Sometimes they would stay in the same hotel on business, but it was always professional and most definitely separate rooms. By then, Marlayna knew that Victor was a widower with a small son. The way Victor spoke of his late wife, she knew that she could never compete. Victor had clearly adored his wife, and no woman on earth could possibly take the place of his beloved Lydia. Marlayna had to contend herself with being a friend, purely platonic, but always loyal, and always available to help out if required.

Marlayna had settled in North London, after divorcing her English and very bombastic husband. She was delighted that Victor had recently moved to the area too. She had grown to love Jonny, Victor's son he was a beautiful boy. She had watched him grow up from a beautiful young boy into a handsome young man. She watched him now, with the beautiful girl, he had just introduced her to, and as they went off in search of Victor, she thought wistfully that she hoped she would be part of their lives for many more years to come.

Sarah had expected the house to be filled with priceless antiques. All very tasteful, but a bit stuffy, like living in a museum. She was pleasantly surprised to be proved wrong. The house was light, bright and very tastefully furnished, but in a modern style. The walls had all been painted white, and there were large modern black leather sofas in the living room.

Chrome and glass coffee tables were dotted around the large room, and a modern chrome and glass chandelier hung from the high ceiling. A very beautiful grey marble fireplace dominated one wall, and a huge colourful geometric canvas was displayed above it. There were some black and white photographs on the mantelpiece, in silver frames of a stunningly beautiful woman who Sarah guessed must have been Jonny's mother. She had Jonny's beautiful eyes. Sarah felt quite choked up seeing them, knowing that she had died so young. They photographs fitted in beautifully amongst the modern feel of the room, as the frames were contemporary and the black and white images were very striking. The only things in the room that were not contemporary were the contents of a glass display cabinet that stood in a corner. It was filled with tin plate toys and tin soldiers' .They were very attractive and colourful, and somehow did not look out of place. They added a welcome splash of colour. There were several more art works around the wall to break up the white walls. Sarah loved the room. It was stylish yet homely.

The house was crowded with chattering guests, and Jonny led Sarah by the hand to seek out his father.

Victor Mason held out his hand to Sarah and smiled. He looked like an older more distinguished version of Jonny. She shook his hand shyly, but smiled back. Her smile lit up her beautiful young face. Victor liked her instantly. He knew his son was mad about this young lady, he hadn't stopped talking about her since they met, and now he could see the attraction. She was a stunning girl, but it was more than that. She had a warmth and charm about her, and he trusted his son's instincts. He looked at his son's anxious face, and winked. He saw Jonny visibly relax, then. He had always needed his dad's approval, and Victor was usually only too willing to give it. They had always had a very relaxed relationship. Jonny had been a lovely little boy, happy and outgoing with a mischievous sense of humour. He had not changed, really, as he had grown up. Victor's heart swelled with pride when he looked at his son and his eyes were full of love. He had been a bit miffed he had to admit, when Jonny had missed the auction on the day he had spotted Sarah in the street. However, when he had come home, he had been so animated when he told Victor that he had met the girl of his dreams, Victor had instantly forgiven him. He had felt exactly the same way when he had met Lydia, Jonny's mother.

The introductions were suddenly interrupted by a large chocolate brown Labrador, who came bumbling towards them, his rudder like tail thumping wildly at the sight of Jonny and Sarah. Sarah was delighted. She had met Truffle before and loved him. She forgot all her intentions to be on her best behaviour and bent down to stroke his velvety ears and give him a kiss. Victor smiled at Jonny. Any girl who loved animals the way Sarah obviously loved his beloved Truffle was fine in his book. "Hello, Truff! Good boy, have you missed me? I missed you. Yes, you're a lovely boy." She crooned, as the large dog licked her face. "Maybe we can go for another walk soon... I'll get Jonny to take us both to Parliament Hill fields. Yes, you'll like it there, boy.." Jonny and his father watched Sarah with the dog, who they both adored. Victor could see the love in his son's eyes and he beamed. "Well, I can see Truffle has another member for his fan club. Sarah, don't let that mutt monopolise you all night, he is already spoilt rotten! Come on; let me get you another drink"

Sarah stood sipping a vodka and tonic, after Jonny had given her the grand tour of the house and his flat above. She was beginning to relax and enjoy herself. She had loved Jonny's little flat, and could have quite happily stayed up there for the rest of the evening, especially when Jonny had pulled her into his arms and kissed her, but out of politeness, they had reluctantly re-joined the noise and chatter again.

The hideous Louise spotted Sarah standing alone from the safety of the kitchen. Jonny had left Sarah for a few moments to go and get some more drinks. Louise had been watching Jonny dancing with Sarah and been eaten up with jealousy. Jonny had finally left his little shop girl's side! At last! The two of them had practically been joined at the hip all evening. She seized her chance and came striding towards Sarah.

Oh good thought Sarah sarcastically, Louise whatsit-thingummy, this time minus her horse faced pal. Why couldn't she just bugger off and leave her and Jonny in peace? Maybe Louise wanted a nice chat, as her pal, young horse face was busy with a nosebag, eating a bale of hay. Ha, fat chance Sarah mused.

Sarah was sure she had just heard the pal whinnying in the kitchen. Oh lord, hadn't Jonny said that the horrible Louise wanted to be his girlfriend? No wonder she was so spitefully jealous. Sarah was competition. She decided to try to be charitable. After all, she would be the one snuggling up with Jonny later, and this Louise was just a kid, really, she was still at school. Jonny had gone to the kitchen in search of vodka and Sarah hoped he would not be gone long. She didn't know how long she could maintain her charitable mood for. She was sure she had felt Louise giving her the evil eye when she had been dancing with Jonny earlier.

Louise had a look on her face of pure hatred. Obviously not after a polite little chat, Sarah told herself grimly. She was not even trying to hide it, either, but Sarah remained calm. Brace yourself, she thought. Louise Whatsit-thingummy pinned a false smile to her over made up face and in a voice that could cut glass, said to Sarah "Hello, aren't you Jonny's latest squeeze? I'm Louise, a VERY good friend of Jon's. We go WAY back."

Sarah tried not to smile at the way Miss Double Barrel had emphasised the words "very good friend" All the time she spoke she was eyeing Sarah up. Sarah felt herself bristle, but smiled her sweetest smile. She felt her charitable intentions evaporate.

 "Oh hello there!" Sarah said with heavy sarcasm, "Yes, I'm Sarah, Jonny's girlfriend." Sarah emphasised the word "girlfriend" in the same way that Louise had emphasised the word "very." Louise looked furious. Point one to me, Sarah told herself before continuing, "I know who you are, darling!. Jonny told me you had a bit of a school girl crush on him." Sarah was gratified to see miss posh pants blanche. Out of the corner of her eye, she saw Truffle sneakily help himself to a chicken vol au vont that someone had carelessly left unattended on one of the glass and chrome coffee tables.

 Miss posh pants was gearing up for another verbal volley. "I may be still at school, but I happen to have more than a few brain cells in MY head. I am getting an education. Aren't you just a shop girl?" she said viciously. Really, she was an amateur at this, thought Sarah. She wasn't going to rise to the bait. She had had plenty of practise dealing with snotty customers. Calmly she replied, "Yes lovey, I am a shop girl. I really enjoy it actually, and my education included learning good manners, and being polite to people. Aren't you just a spoiled little brat who thinks she's so much cleverer than she really is, and is totally pissed off because I'm going out with the bloke she fancies? Lighten up, love, go and stuff your face with a few of those delicious sausage rolls and find a bloke of your own"

Sarah heard Jonny laughing. She had not noticed him come back. He was behind her, with a tray. On it were two drinks and yet another plate piled high with food, including what was left of her mum's sausage rolls. He had promised Marlayna that he would get her a plate of goodies from the kitchen. Miss posh pants had turned a lovely shade of puce, and Sarah almost felt sorry for her. Jonny carefully placed the tray down on a coffee table beside Sarah.

Louise was wearing a pair of very tight dazzling white trousers that clung to her ample backside, and had teamed the skin tight trousers with a low cut red top.

She had obviously made a real but misguided effort to impress. She had been trying to look sexy but had only achieved a look akin to a cheap hooker. She would have been attractive if it was not for her too tarty clothes and spiteful nature, thought Sarah. Whatever it was she was studying at that posh school of hers, it was not fashion, style or good taste. Her clothes were no doubt expensive, but were too tight and way too revealing. Jonny leaned over Sarah's shoulder, putting his arms around Sarah's waist. He was grinning at Louise, enjoying her squirm. She really was a pain in the arse, he thought. How dare she upset Sarah like that?

"Touché, I think," he said, looking pleased. He was delighted that Sarah had given as good as she got. She was quite a girl. He had heard every word, and he loved Sarah's spirit. "You're too late with the sausage rolls, I'm afraid, I've already scoffed most of them. I think you forgot my dad is a shopkeeper. So am I, come to think of it, as I work for my dad. Nothing wrong in working in a shop or eating sausage rolls. Good, honest grub, and shop people are the salt of the earth! I think you owe us an apology, young Loo…."

Truffle had finished his vol au vont in one gulp, and had decided to try his luck with Jonny, who was standing near a deliciously smelling plate of goodies. Truffle's nose quivered in anticipation, his mouth watering. He licked his lips and sat beside him, looking hopefully at the tray on the coffee table. His thick tail waggled from side to side as he sat.

Louise looked at the eager dog in disgust, and began flapping her arms as if a swarm of flies had suddenly descended, much to Sarah and Jonny's amusement.   A line of drool had formed at the side of Truffle's mouth. Sarah never trusted anyone who did not like dogs. She had warmed to Jonny even more when he had told her all about his big daft dog on their second date. Sarah had always loved animals. She still had fond memories of Suki the cat who lived in the sweet shop where her mum worked when she was a little girl. She had always wanted a pet of her own, but no pets were allowed in the flats where she had grown up. She loved meeting Jonny for walks with Truffle in the evening after work now that the nights were light.

"Get him away!" Louise said angrily, as Truffle wagged his tail excitedly. "What on earth is he doing running around in a house full of guests, anyway? Can't you keep him locked out in the garden or something?" Truffle, seeing a good game in the making, watched her flapping arms with interest. Hoping the arm flapping game might include food, he barked excitedly, and leapt to his feet putting an encouraging paw on miss posh pants immaculate white trousers. The drool on his mouth flew off as he shook his head eagerly, and landed on Louise's sparkling white trousers.

They were now no longer immaculate as, unfortunately, Truffle had also stepped in a puddle of spilled red wine as he went to investigate the arm waving game. A frantic guest was on their hands and knees beside Truffle, furiously rubbing at the stain with a napkin. A dirty red paw mark appeared instantly on Posh pants trouser leg, slightly south of the drool. Sarah bit her lips and tried not to laugh. Jonny grabbed Truffle's collar, to stop him leaping on Louise again, but Louise had stepped backwards. As she did so, she turned her ankle in her platform-soled shoes, and fell flat on her arse, landing in an ungainly heap on the polished wooden floor.

 A plate of half-eaten canapés that someone had carelessly left on the floor broke her fall. Truffle leapt forward, jerking himself out of Jonny's grasp, and began greedily wolfing down the squashed canapés that were now imbedded on posh pants trousers .He was also helping himself to the contents of Jonny's plate, as he had nudged the coffee table and knocked some of the food onto the floor when Truffle had jerked forward.

Watching and listening, it was Suzy who burst out laughing first. She had been talking to Billy on the other side of the room, but had not missed a trick. Then it seemed like the whole room joined in. Truffle was of course oblivious to the noise, he was far too busy focusing on gobbling down as much as he could. This was turning out to be a good party for greedy brown Labradors.

If only Louise had joined in, and been able to laugh it off, it would have been all right. Sarah held out her hand to help posh pants up, but she ignored her, scrambled to her feet, and fled the room without a word. Victor Mason heard the commotion from the kitchen and came to see what was going on. "Everything okay?" he asked Jonny anxiously. "Yeah, don't worry, dad" Jonny said. "I think Louise has just had a bit too much to drink."

"She's drunk already? It's not 9'0' clock yet" Victor said incredulously.

"It does seem a bit…vulgar" Sarah chipped in mischievously.

Louise stood in the hall, feeling totally humiliated. Trying to regain her composure, she blinked away her tears and thought she would have to ring for a taxi and go home. She could not even go back into the throng to let her friend Camilla know she was leaving. Blow Camilla, she thought. Let her work it out for herself. She could find her own way home. She fumbled in her bag for the card that she always kept with the local cab firm's number. She lived in the Barbican during term time. Her mother sometimes stayed with her, as she worked near Moorgate and it was so convenient, but sometimes she had the flat to herself. Not bad for a seventeen year old, she told herself smugly. She was doing her A levels at The City of London School for girls. It was an expensive private girl's school on the exclusive Barbican Estate. Her parents had a large house in Highgate but also had a small Pied a Terre. It was just two minutes from school. She was the envy of her school friends. Well, most of them. There were the girls who had parents that owned most of the Home Counties of course, and also had flats in the Barbican. Louise put down the receiver after curtly demanding a taxi as soon as possible.

As she hung up, Louise spotted Jonny's keys in the Royal Doulton bowl besides the phone. She recognised his distinctive key ring. It had a photograph of his bloody stupid drooling dog on it. Smiling to herself, and looking around casually to make sure no one was looking, she picked up the keys and slipped them into her handbag. She opened the front door quietly and stepped outside to wait for her cab.

Suzy had managed to get very drunk at the party. She hadn't meant to, but after the fiasco with that posh little brat, she had a large drink and a laugh about it with Sarah, then some music was put on, and she had a bit of a dance and another drink, and another and another. She was trying to pluck up the courage to tell Billy she did not want to go out with him anymore, but somehow she could not quite manage it. The trouble was, the more she drank the more attractive Billy became. He really was a good-looking swine. Finally, Billy had said it was about time he took her home before she embarrassed herself. She did not argue. She did not remember much about staggering off down the road holding on to Billy's arm, or saying goodbye to Sarah or Jonny. She vaguely remembered being very sick when she got home. Luckily, Billy had gone by then. She had remembered that they had had sex in King Square Park though. It had seemed really funny to climb over the locked gates to get inside, and to do it on a park bench. She did not remember climbing back out of the park again, and she certainly did not remember Billy taking all of her money out of her purse whilst she had been distracted rearranging her clothes, and slyly putting her money into his own wallet.

Carrie had settled herself down on the sofa after Sarah went off to her party at Jonny's house. If there was nothing much to watch on the telly, she had a good book to read, and a bag of mint imperials to polish off. She was looking forward to a pleasant evening. She had just got herself comfy, reading the radio times before picking up her book, when the phone rang. It had been the ward sister at the hospital. The sister had told her in a delighted voice, obviously thinking she was imparting very good news that Tommy was sitting up in bed, and tomorrow they would be getting him up to start physiotherapy.

Sarah was surprised to see her mum still up when she got home from the party. It had been very late, and she had not expected her mum to wait up. Jonny had walked her home, but had not come inside, not wanting to disturb Carrie. Carrie looked up as Sarah came in, and smiled when she saw her daughter's happy face. She had obviously had a wonderful time. She looked forward to hearing all about it. Jonny had been so good for her daughter. She had never seen her more animated and glad to be alive. How lovely she looked, with her whole life ahead of her, and so in love. Her own face hid her anguish at the earlier phone call. It had been kind of the ward sister to call, she had obviously thought she was being thoughtful, keeping Carrie informed on Tommy's progress.

Tommy was obviously getting stronger. One day, perhaps soon, he would be allowed home. She knew that the hospital expected her to care for him and thought as his loving wife, she would do it all willingly. Carrie had become used to the new carefree life without him. How could she go back to living under his shadow when he came home again for good?

Suzy had the hangover from hell after the party. She had not gone in to work on Monday morning. Her mum Joycie had rung Sarah at 7.30a.m to tell Sarah not to wait for her. Suzy she said was still in bed and had been sick all weekend. Sarah had not looked forward to a day at work without Suzy. It wasn't nearly as much fun on her own.

Miss Parish appeared just after 9'O'clock. "No Suzy today?" she asked Sarah. "Er....no, Miss Parish" Sarah said slightly nervously, "She has a.. tummy bug. Her mum said she had been ill all over the weekend. Her mum did ring the office number to let you know"

Eleanor Parish was not fooled for a second. She smiled ruefully at Sarah. "Oh, yes, I'm sure she did ring, don't worry, she's not in any trouble. Good party was it?" she added quietly. Sarah could not help herself she blushed crimson. "It's all right, I was young once, you know. So long as our Miss Pond doesn't make a habit of it."

Sarah looked relieved. She was all right, was Miss Parish. Quite attractive really, for an older woman, she thought charitably. Sarah wondered why she had never married. It wasn't the sort of thing she could ask, obviously, but the girls on the shop floor gossiped of course. Word was that Eleanor Parish had been let down very badly by the love of her life when she was in her twenties, and had never been romantically involved ever again. She had instead, decided to concentrate on her career, and had risen from sales assistant to shop floor manager over the years. She had had to work twice as hard as any man to get herself taken seriously, but she had managed it. She was a liked and well respected member of the team and had earned the respect of all of the other staff members. She was proud to eat in the senior staff member's exclusive dining hall every day, and be listened to attentively at board meetings. It had been a long hard fought battle.

Eleanor Parish had been in love with her school friend, Ruby Drake. The two girls had been lovers ever since school and Eleanor would have happily followed Ruby to the ends of the earth and back again, if she had been asked to by her beloved Ruby. It had caused a scandal of course. The school had been out raged, and Eleanor and Ruby had been asked to leave before completing their A levels. Her family had disowned Eleanor, but she had happily given up everything for Ruby. They had moved into a tiny one bedroom flat together and been blissfully happy. Ruby's family had been a little more liberal and although they had not exactly embraced the situation, they did learn to accept the two girls as a couple and had helped to support Ruby financially until the girls were settled. Eleanor had found a job in Debenhams, and Ruby had found work in a little coffee shop. They did not have much money, and had to scrape by, but Eleanor had never been happier. They lived in that little flat for ten years, and Eleanor had worked hard and never missed a day at work. They had decorated and improved their home together, and bought furniture and paintings to make it theirs. They had been saving to get a deposit so that they could buy their first house together.

One day, Eleanor had come home unexpectedly early from work with a migraine. It was the first time in ten years that she had ever taken any time off sick. She had tried to see the day out, but her supervisor had spotted her looking deathly pale in the staff toilet and had said she should go home early for once.

 Eleanor had reluctantly agreed, as she had really felt dreadful. She put her key in the door and headed for the bedroom. All she wanted was to lie down in a darkened room. As she opened the bedroom door, she heard frantic scrambling from the other side of the door. She found Ruby in bed with another woman. Not just any woman either, but a neighbour she had considered a friend.

Eleanor had never recovered from the betrayal and had quite literally fallen to pieces. She had to take time off work and had even spent time in a psychiatric ward after trying clumsily to slash her wrists. Her manager on the shop floor, whilst not knowing all the details, had still been wonderfully understanding. When Eleanor was ready to return to work, she had devoted herself to her job. Slowly she had gained confidence and had earned her promotion. Now she had her own little house on the outskirts of London, and was quite content on her own. She had her cats, Bobby and Blue for company. Her work was her love now and that was all she needed. She realised that she had become a cliché of a lonely old lesbian, living with her cats, but she did not really mind. She was, for the most part, content. At least, that is what she told herself.

Sarah and Jonny had taken Truffle to Parliament Hill fields for a picnic, and were now driving home. Jonny had driven them in the small white van that he and his father used for transporting antiques. Truffle was curled up fast asleep on his blanket in the back of the van. They had had a wonderful time, and Truffle was worn out. "Look at that dopey dog" Sarah said fondly, "Someone should tell him that for a retriever, he lets the side down. I ran and fetched that ball far more than he did"

"Truffle doesn't do fetching" Jonny said, grinning. "If you want it, you have to get it yourself. Truff is far more interested in eating. I think he must have eaten half the sticks in Parliament Hill. It's a miracle they've got any trees left!"

Jonny parked the van and Sarah got wearily out and closed the passenger door, whilst Jonny encouraged a sleepy Truffle to leave his comfortable blanket and jump out of the back of the van.

Jonny's dad was away this weekend buying antiques at a fair in Dorset. He had left Jonny in charge of the shop and Truffle. Today was Sunday, and Jonny had promised to cook a meal for Sarah after their day out. Sarah had been most impressed that Jonny not only had his own flat in his father's house, but that he could cook as well. Jonny had laughed at how impressed Sarah had been, and told her that he had learned how to cook from an early age because his dad was useless in the kitchen, and it had been a question of cook or starve. He had promised her a full Sunday roast, and had a leg of lamb waiting for them in his fridge. Sarah was pleasantly tired after their day out, and was looking forward to a lazy evening being waited on and cooked for by the delectable Jonny.

After dinner, if they had the energy, they were going to put on some records, roll back the rug and dance the night away. Sarah had been delighted when Jonny had suggested it. She loved to dance. She could think of few things nicer than being in the arms of her lovely Jon listening to their favourite songs.

Truffle made for his bowl of water as soon as the front door opened. Sarah and Jonny heard him lap noisily even before the front door closed. Usually after a long walk, Truffle would dunk his head in his water bowl, drip water all over the kitchen floor, then settle down for a nice long nap. Today, however, he lifted his dripping head from his bowl, sniffed the air and began to growl. This was so unusual; Jonny frowned, and said, "What is it, boy?"

Still growling, Truffle ran to the bottom of the stairs, looked up towards Jonny's flat and began barking and wagging his tail excitedly. It was then that they heard a bump. Very faint, but definitely coming from overhead. "Someone's up there," Jonny whispered to Sarah, as he began to creep as quietly as he could up the stairs. "Don't go up there!" Sarah said, panic stricken, but following closely behind. Truffle raced past the pair of them, and used his head to barge Jonny's door open. Jonny was only seconds behind, and Sarah stood on the stairs, waiting to see who or what was there.

Louise Blakely Green was lying on top of Jonny's bed. She was naked, and did not look very pleased to see Truffle, who was now sniffing her excitedly and wagging his entire body, creating quite a draught. Jonny let out a surprised " Woh!" noise, and Louise tried to desperately shoo away the excited Labrador and cover up her naked body. She had not received quite the reception she had been hoping for. "Christ, Louise, what the hell are you playing at?" Jonny said angrily, when he had recovered from the shock. Sarah heard the commotion from the top of the stairs, but was still out of sight. "I..thought I'd surprise you" Louise said, trying to sound sexy and she hoped, alluring. She smiled her sexiest smile in Jonny's direction. "You did that all right" Jonny said quietly, then added quickly, " cover yourself up" Louise had laid back down on the bed, letting go of the bed cover, as Truffle had now lost interest and was making himself comfortable on the bedroom carpet. She put her arms above her head and pointed her pert little breasts in Jonny's direction. Jonny looked away, embarrassed. Louise was not giving up that easily.

"Come on, Jonny, don't be like that. I'm here, and I'm all yours." Sarah, hearing this, wanted to rush in and slap the little slut until her teeth rattled. She was so shocked however that she found herself rooted to the spot, unable to move. She listened instead in grim fascination, as Jonny said quietly "Get dressed, Louise, and go home."

Sarah heard Louise start to cry. "Please…Jonny…." She begged, between sobs. Sarah blushed right down to her toes. Did this girl have no self-respect? She heard Jonny's voice, softer now; say firmly "Look Louise, nothing is ever going to happen between us. Not now, not ever. I'm sorry, but you have to understand that. I have a girlfriend, you know that, and I happen to love her very much, but even if I didn't have a girlfriend, you are far too young for me. It just wouldn't work" he spoke gently, but he had to get it through to her that he just was not interested. Sarah, still listening on the stairs, felt her heart turn over.

He had said he loved her! He could easily have got angry, and totally humiliated the little cow, but he was being so kind. Much kinder than she felt right now! She had finally regained the power to move, and quietly stepped into the doorway. Louise's eyes widened in shock as she realised Sarah had witnessed the entire show. Jonny turned around as Sarah said curtly "How the hell did you get in here, anyway?"

Jonny had called a cab to take the still tearful Louise home. Sarah had remained remarkably calm under the circumstances, especially when Louise had admitted to stealing Jonny's keys at the party. He had been searching everywhere for them, and had eventually had to get another set cut. The house seemed incredibly quiet now Louise had finally gone. Sarah was sitting on a kitchen stool, In Jonny's little flat, watching Jonny peel potatoes for their dinner. She was still trying to calm down. It wasn't every day she saw a naked teenager in her boyfriends bed. She hoped it was an experience that would not be repeated any time soon.

It had taken her a long time to trust Jonny when they had started dating; she had not wanted to let her guard down and risk being hurt. Now, here she was, finding a naked teenager in his bed. Despite herself, there was a nagging doubt eating away at her. Jonny had told Louise that he loved Sarah, but...did he really mean it? Would he have turned Louise down if Sarah had not been there? She wanted to believe him when he reassured her, but her doubts would not totally go away. Like a malevolent little demon, the doubts crept onto her shoulder and whispered to her. They fed her insecurities while she lay in her bed at night, eating and knawing away at her happiness. She tried to keep them at bay but a naked Louise had set the demons dancing again in delight.

The meal, despite everything, had been delicious. Truffle was now sound asleep and snoring on Jonny's bed, after wolfing down some lamb scraps that Jonny had saved for him after carving the roast. Poor Jonny had spent ages apologising for Louise, whilst he cooked it and got more and more flustered trying to convince Sarah that he did not have feelings for Louise. In the end, Sarah had had to put him out of his misery. Despite still having slight worries inside her head, she had kissed him. She mentally muffled the nagging harpies in her head and said "It's fine, Jon, I believe you. Now, did you mean what you said when you told slut girl that you loved me?" she smiled mischievously as she watched Jonny squirm in embarrassment. It was nice to turn the tables on him for once and see him squirm a little bit. "Oh hell, you heard that too, huh?" Jonny said, pulling Sarah into his arms.

"Oh yes. I heard everything" Sarah leaned back, still smiling mischievously, and looking into Jonny's beautiful but mortally embarrassed face. She wanted so badly to trust him, and she could see the love in his eyes as he looked at her. Maybe it was time to stop worrying, she told herself.

"Well, yes, I did mean it. I love you, Sarah Miller," he said softly, kissing her gently. He looked into her eyes as he held her, and Sarah saw such love and tenderness on his face that her heart melted. She realised in that moment that if she did not trust this wonderful man, she would never be able to trust anyone, and she suddenly felt free for the first time in her life. Free and so elated and happy that she wanted to run out into the street and shout to the world that she was in love.

Jonny held her close again, and with his voice thick with emotion, he murmured into the nape of her neck "You're in my heart, and my blood. I will always love you, so there. In fact, I don't bloody care if I come home and find a thousand naked girls in my bed, I wouldn't look at any of them, because they wouldn't be a patch on you. Now, if I was to come home and find you naked in my bed... ow!" he had to stop, because Sarah was giggling, and had thumped him with the oven glove that was on the table. He started to laugh, and begged for mercy. "Well now, Jonny boy, play your cards right and I might just make your dreams come true...lets skip the washing up...."

Sarah had been remarkably relaxed in Jonny's arms, and in his bed. She had been a virgin until she met Jonny, and was so glad she had waited. She had expected to be a nervous fumbling wreck. She had read all sorts of romantic fiction, and did not think for one minute that real life could ever be like that. She thought sex would be painful the first time. Messy, yucky and not something she would be too keen to repeat. That was before she had met Jonny, of course. She was so happy to be proved wrong. She had trusted Jonny, it had been quite easy once she put her mind to it, and trusted her instincts and he had been so gentle, she had been overwhelmed. All the tosh she had ever read had not prepared her for the intensity of love that she had felt when he looked into her eyes and smiled at her. She had surprised even herself. Her skin had tingled when he touched her, and she realised that she had never desired any one before, not like this, anyway. It was a new and quite wonderful sensation. She had not felt shy, she had not fumbled, and it had been beautiful. When it was over, they had cuddled together, and Sarah had never felt happier or gladder to be alive. When Jonny fell asleep, she lay for ages, just gazing at his beautiful peaceful face and his lovely long eyelashes. She gently kissed his cheek, and wished with all her heart that she could lock out the real world and remain here, in this moment forever.

Louise had been given a Kodak Instamatic camera for her thirteenth birthday. It was still in good nick, and came in very handy for taking saucy photographs that she wanted to keep away from prying eyes. She managed to persuade Camilla to take some topless shots of her one evening after school. She was still smarting from Jonny's latest rebuff, but was determined to make him see just what a catch she would be. It was only a matter of time, she told herself. The stupid shop girl must be getting close to her expiry date soon. Louise was eager to step in and take her place. She looked at the topless photographs of herself. Some of them were quite explicit, almost as good as the ones she had seen in her father's grubby magazines. She thought she looked incredibly sexy in one or two shots. Smiling, she picked the two best ones, put them in an envelope and wrote Jonny's name and address on it. She grabbed her door keys and walked hurriedly to the post box.

Billy Jameson was in deep doggy doo doo and he knew it. He wondered how he had managed to be so bloody stupid. He really envied his mate Jonny, and, although he did not like to admit it, not even to himself, he was jealous of him. Jonny had everything handed to him on a plate. He had a rich dad who doted on him, his own flat in his dad's big posh house, and a gorgeous classy bird.

That Sarah was so sexy; Billy would have loved to try it on with her. He knew better than to mess with her sort, though. He had a good thing going with Jonny; he was not daft enough to mess that up. Ever since he had first met Jonny he had been cultivating him, and had worked hard to gain his trust.

Jonny might be a posh spoilt git, but he was a good mate. He would always lend him money, too, and never asked for it back. He needed money now. He had though he could keep his gambling under control, and it had been such a buzz at first. Winning was amazing but it was when he almost won, but didn't, that he really felt the adrenaline pumping. The excitement, the anticipation of what might be...oh man, there was no high quite like it. It was better than sex, better than drugs even, but then he had run out of money, as he always did, and had started borrowing. First, he had borrowed from his younger brother Graham. Graham had lent him the odd tenner here or there but when Billy had forgotten to pay him back, Graham had told him in no uncertain terms to go and get stuffed. That was when Billy had taken money from the cash float at work. It had been okay at first, he had not been caught. It was only the odd tenner here or there, and he had managed

to put the money back when the Gee Gee's romped home.
George, his boss at the garage, had not rumbled him. But now...
he had lost every last penny he had, and had borrowed from
Nick Crowley.

 Nasty Nick was a loan shark who operated on the Packington
Estate where Billy still lived. Everybody knew Nick. Most people
were wise enough not to tangle with him. Those stupid or
desperate enough to mess with him ended up with their legs
broken or worse. Billy had panicked when George had noticed
that money was missing. Billy had lied, and told George that he
had taken it to get parts for a car he was working on. Of course,
then he needed the money to actually buy the parts, or else be
rumbled. That was when he bumped into Nick Crowley. He had
borrowed £100. He had promised to pay it back in a week. It
was a lot of money to borrow. A small fortune. How could he
have been so bloody stupid? He had only taken £50 from the
float at work, but had hoped at the time to win big and solve all
his problems, paying Nick back, paying off all his outstanding
debts, and maybe even have a little holiday. He always got
carried away dreaming. Suzy had been nagging him for ages;
she had been very fed up lately saying that he never took her
anywhere any more. She was getting bored, he could tell. Birds
like Suzy were expensive, they needed to be taken out and
shown a good time.

It was payday and he convinced himself he would give the
money straight to Nick Crowley. He had put in a lot of overtime
and had earned a lot more than usual this month. Then on his
way, he had seen Tyler Morgan coming out of the betting shop.
He had given Billy a dead cert.Tyler had a friend who was a
jockey. Billy had his wages all counted out in his wallet, ready to
hand over to Nick. He would be skint until next payday, but he

told himself it would be worth it. He would pay off all he owed, and stop having to look over his shoulder all the time. He tried to walk past the betting shop, had reached as far as the corner, but it was as if a bloody magnet was pulling him back. He kept telling himself if this dead cert came up, he could double even triple his wages, and he would be laughing all the way to the bank.

He could pay off Nick, take Suzy somewhere special and maybe have some left over. He felt the old familiar tingle of excitement and anticipation flowing through his veins. He swore that he could feel the money in his wallet digging into his ribs, urging him on. He licked his lips, pushed open the betting shop door and stepped inside.

It was a shame the horse had turned out to have only three bloody legs. Billy had felt sick. All his hard-earned cash was gone, just like that. He had ended up staying all afternoon, trying to win back something, but it had definitely not been his day.

Now Nick was demanding the money back with interest, and the interest was rising daily. On top of that, George was getting suspicious, as the irate customer still didn't have his car back, owing to the fact that the parts it needed still hadn't materialised. Billy panicked. He had no choice. He would have to go cap in hand and see Jonny.

Tommy Miller was making good progress with the physiotherapy. His speech was still slightly slurred, but at least he could speak.His face still looked distorted and his left arm and leg dragged a little, but the doctor had told him that, at this rate, he would be able to go home very soon. Carrie sat at

Tommy's bedside, looking up at the earnest young medic. She tried her best to look pleased, but could not quite manage it.

It was Friday lunchtime, and Sarah and Suzy had just sat down in the staff restaurant with a plateful of fish and chips each. The fish and chips they dished up in the staff restaurant were far better than any you could buy at the chippy, and it was a fraction of the price, too. It had become a weekly treat that both girls looked forward to. "I suppose you're seeing Jonny tonight?" Suzy said a little enviously, as she splashed vinegar on to her chips.

"Yes, I certainly am" Sarah said happily, drowning her piece of fish with tartare sauce. She saw Suzy's odd expression, and added "Suze, are you alright?"

"I s'pose so. It's just that I'm bored. Billy never has any money to take me out these days, and he always seems edgy and short tempered. I'm getting really fed up! I should've dumped him weeks ago, but I couldn't pluck up the courage. I dunno what he does with his dosh. He earns a decent wage at the garage, he's been doing loads of overtime too, but he's always skint. He even asks me to lend him money every pay day!" Sarah didn't tell Suzy that Billy had asked Jonny to lend him money, too. She had overheard him practically begging Jonny to lend him a thousand pounds just a few days ago. A thousand pounds! Who did he think Jonny was, Rockefeller?

Billy hadn't known Sarah was there, she had been upstairs in Jonny's bed room when Billy arrived unexpectedly. She had not let on that she had heard the heated conversation, which had ended when Jonny had said sorry, but he didn't have that kind of money. Sarah had heard the door slam and seen Billy stomp off angrily from Jonny's bedroom window. Jonny had just said

Billy had come to give his dad an invoice for his car that had recently been serviced. Sarah admired Jonny's loyalty to his friend, but did not like being lied to. She really had begun to trust Jonny, but she was not happy about his blinkered view of Billy.

It was the one thing they constantly disagreed about. Jonny would not have a word said against Billy, and Sarah got frustrated because she knew in her heart that Billy was bad news. She tried to put it out of her mind and concentrate on Suzy.

She looked at her troubled friend and smiled as she said, "Well, you know what you've always told me, if it stops being fun, it's time to cut and run. If you're bored, why don't you give him the elbow? It's not like you to be backwards in coming forward, Suze. Dump him and get it over with."

"I can't"

"Why? It's not worth hanging around if you're not happy." Sarah hoped with all her heart that Suzy would see the light and dump Billy. The more Sarah saw of Billy, the less she liked him. She was irritated too, that Jonny always defended him, and would not hear a word said against him. She didn't think Billy deserved his loyalty. She had heard about boys from the Packington estate all through her school days, they were a rough lot, and always in trouble with the law.

Suzy had told her miserably that on the way home from Victor's party she had managed to lose all the money from her purse, almost £15. Sarah had wondered if Billy had taken it. She looked up from her plate at Suzy's anxious face.

Suzy speared a chip viciously onto her fork, before saying quietly, "It's not that simple anymore. I'm pregnant"

CHAPTER FOUR

Billy had popped round to Jonny's flat before work. He knew Jonny would be on his own, as his dad Victor was away at an auction. Billy was on the scrounge. Jonny opened the front door with the days post in his hands. He was munching a piece of toast, and looked surprised to see Billy so early in the morning. He beckoned Billy inside and they went upstairs to Jonny's flat.

Billy sat on the bar stool in Jonny's kitchen, trying to find the right words to extricate the maximum amount of cash from Jonny without it sounding too desperate. Jonny was listening, but opening his post at the same time. Suddenly, he let out a "Holy shit!"

"What is it?" Billy said.

"Christ, that girl never gives up, does she?" he slid the instamatic photos across the counter towards Billy. Billy looked at the naked images of Louise and his eyes nearly popped out of his head. She had certainly left nothing to the imagination. Subtlety was definitely not this little tarts forte.

"Wow! Nice boobs..er..body. She's handing herself to you on a ruddy plate, Jon. Are you sure you're not interested?" Billy realised immediately that he had spoken out of turn as he saw Jonny's angry expression. "No I'm definitely not interested! I wish I'd never clapped eyes on the silly little girl. Get rid of these, please. If Sarah ever came across them, she would go mad. No, on second thoughts' give them to me." Jonny scooped up the offensive pictures and tossed them angrily in to the pedal bin. "More coffee? Anyway, what can I do for you at this ungodly hour?"

Billy had finally plucked up the courage and asked Jonny if he could borrow five hundred pounds. He had been extremely unimpressed when Jonny had sheepishly said he was sorry, but he could not afford that kind of money. He actually offered him fifty. What an insult! Nick Crowley would laugh in his face at that. Billy had had to grit his teeth though, smile and say thanks that would be fine. It would have to do for now. Jonny had said he would go to the bank at lunchtime and had told him to help himself to some more coffee. Then he had disappeared into the bathroom to brush his teeth. As soon as Billy heard the bathroom door lock, he retrieved the photographs from the bin.

Jonny had the tap running. He had not heard Billy slip into his bedroom and strategically hide the photographs of the naked Louise in the drawer on his bedside cabinet.

Sarah was surprised to see Billy when she stepped off the 73 bus after work. She had to walk past the garage; they now had a branch at the Angel as well as Highbury corner. Usually at this time of day, Billy had already gone home. She usually rode all the way home on the bus with Suzy, but had got off the bus before their usual stop this evening as she was meeting Jonny. They were going out for a meal and then on to the pictures. She was going to get changed at Jonny's house tonight. Jonny would meet her on the next corner. Suzy was supposed to be meeting Billy later so she wanted to go home and get ready. She had not told Sarah that she was going to end things with Billy, just in case her nerve failed her.

"Well fancy seeing you here!" Billy said with a grin as Sarah walked by.

"Yes, aren't I the lucky one?" Sarah said with heavy sarcasm. Billy bristled. The stuck up little cow! She had always looked down her nose at him, as if she was somehow a better class of person. She grew up on a poxy council estate too, so he didn't know why she was so high and mighty. He had been waiting for her. He was sure she had been putting the boot in and poisoning Jonny's mind against him. Jonny had never refused to lend him money before she came along. Billy smiled at Sarah, ignoring her sarcastic reply. "Had any more unexpected visits from gorgeous naked young girls lately?" he said casually. Her expression was all the reward he wanted. "What are you talking about?" Sarah jumped in quickly. Ah, he knew she'd bite. "You know what I'm talking about, darling. The lovely Louise! Gave our Jonny a right eyeful, so I heard! Bet she made his day!" he leered at Sarah and she felt her flesh creep. She felt betrayed that Jonny had actually told Billy about it. She was furious that Billy obviously loved every minute of her discomfort. She was even more furious with herself, when the malevolent little demons began nagging at her once again. She struggled to compose herself. "Yes, the silly cow turned up uninvited, but Jonny soon got rid of her." She said with as much dignity as she could muster.

"Are you sure she was uninvited? "

"What are you getting at? Don't stir things, Billy. It ain't funny!"

"I'm not stirring anything, sweetheart. Just saying Louise and Jonny, well, they've got history, that's all. If you don't believe me, you should take a look in Jonny's bedside cabinet. Got some lovely snaps in there. Say's he keeps them close to his bed side to keep him warm at night, if you know what I mean!"

"Sarah wanted to slap Billy, and her face coloured with the effort of trying not to. "My God, Billy, you really are a twisted little bastard aren't you? Jonny has been a really good friend to you, much better than you deserve, and how do you repay him? By trying to shit stir between me and him! What's wrong, Bill? Did you ask for money again, and get a knock back this time? I'm sorry to disappoint you, but I don't believe you! Your little plan hasn't worked! Not every bloke has got a filthy mind like you! I happen to trust Jonny. He's worth a million of blokes like you! Piss off, Bill, and don't ever come near us again!"

Billy's face clouded momentarily. The bitch! He recovered quickly though. "I can see I've touched a nerve, darlin'. You think our Jonny boy would stay faithful? What, when he finds a sexy naked girl in his bed, gagging for it? No man would turn it down! He must've been gutted that you were in the way! Now, if it had been me, I'd have had both of you! A nice threesome would've warmed me up nicely!" Sarah felt herself blush to her toes. Good grief, he was revolting.

"You are disgusting, Billy. The trouble with you is you tend to judge everyone else by your own low standards. Jonny would rather die than stoop to your level. You've lost the best friend you'll ever have, you pathetic little swine. I hope Suzy tells you to get stuffed, too. Now, get out of my bloody way!" Sarah pushed past Billy and stomped off.

Sarah could still hear Billy laughing as she walked off angrily down the street. He had loved winding her up, and she was furious with herself for rising to the bait. The little weasel! She had been right about him all along! She trusted Jon. He would never lie to her or deceive her. Would he?

119

Sarah was so furious that as soon as she saw Jonny she blurted out the whole conversation. Jonny stood silently while Sarah was in full flow. She ended by saying to a stony-faced Jonny "I know he's supposed to be your mate Jon, but he's bad news. He is jealous of you, and he wants to split us up! And don't you dare defend him anymore, cos I won't bloody stand for it!" Jonny reached for Sarah and tried to hold her close. She resisted at first, still too furious to yield, but Jonny held tight to her hand and his eyes told her he wasn't going to give in. "Come here, I'm not going to defend him. I'm just angry with myself I suppose. I really did think he was my friend. No one likes being taken for a mug. I've been such an idiot! All this time, he was playing me like a violin, and I was too stupid to see it" Sarah still resisted Jonny's gaze, but she could feel herself weakening. She saw Jonny's crestfallen face and her anger evaporated. She allowed herself to be enveloped in his arms, still standing on the street corner. She was trembling with emotion, but she so wanted to believe Jonny. In her heart, all her instincts told her she could. The harpies were still flying around her head, but she shot them down.

Jonny held Sarah close to him. He could feel her heart beat and she was shaking with emotion. He did his best to calm her down. His head was reeling with what Sarah had told him. He should have been shocked, but strangely, he wasn't. If he was honest with himself, he had begun to have doubts about Billy himself. He had not wanted to believe the worst but Billy was a manipulative user and this just proved it. Jonny gave Sarah a reassuring squeeze. He stroked her hair soothingly and whispered into her ear softly "Sarah, I would never do anything to hurt you. That little tart Louise sent me some photographs. I threw them straight in the bin, I swear to you. I'm sorry, I should have told you, I realise that now, but I didn't want to upset you.

It meant nothing to me. If they are in my bedside cabinet, Billy put them there. Come home with me now, and I'll show you. I've got nothing to hide. If Billy did do it, he'd better hide, though. Cos when I get my hands on him, I'll ruddy kill him!" As Jonny released Sarah from his arms and kissed her, she said quietly "Not if I find him first"

Jonny opened the drawer and immediately saw the photographs. He went very pale, just closed the drawer and said grimly to Sarah "Wait here"

Sarah had argued, and said she wanted to go too. Jonny had argued back, and told Sarah that she wasn't coming, then added, "Please. I need to see him on my own."

"Why?" Sarah spat out venomously, "Do you two want to get your stories straight?"

"What? Sarah, please! You have to believe me! I would never lie to you! Billy is just a vindictive bastard! He's pissed off, because he wanted money and I said no! I guess I'm no use to him anymore, so he thinks he's got nothing to lose by stirring up trouble! Please trust me..I wouldn't lie to you, Sarah, you mean everything to me.."

"But you already have lied to me! Jon, I heard you and Billy when he came round! You told me he came about a car invoice! You lied! What else have you lied about?" Sarah was crying now. Jonny put his hands through his hair in frustration. He had been such an idiot. He felt panic rising. He was in danger of losing Sarah and he would do anything to avoid that. He banged his fist down on the bedside table in frustration. Sarah let out a shocked gasp, and stepped backwards. Jonny stood up, concerned, and reached out for her. She backed away. Jonny could see fear on her face. Oh God! She couldn't think he would hurt her, surely. "Sarah?" he said softly, "Oh darling, it's all right! What is it?"

"Stay away from me!" she said, a note of hysteria creeping into her voice. She was really crying now. Jonny felt his heart breaking. Bloody hell, what had that bastard of a father done to her? Would she ever trust him? Jonny sat on the bed. "It's okay. Oh sweetheart, I'm so sorry! I would rather cut my own arms off than hurt you" Sarah had given in then. Poor Jonny's face had been desolate. Her own face crumpled and she ran into Jonny's arms. He held her and she sobbed all over his shirt. He let her, softly stroking her hair, until she was calm again. Then he kissed her, and told her he wouldn't be long. She let him go without another word. She waited restlessly, sitting on Jonny's bed with Truffle asleep beside her.

Jonny knew that Billy would be in the Passage public house by now. It was not far from Jonny's house. Just along Upper Street. Billy considered this his local, and popped in after work most days. He was supposed to be meeting Suzy later on in the Golden Hind pub further along the road. He liked to keep Suzy away from his local. He had once winked at Jonny and said he didn't care to mix business with pleasure. Jonny still was not sure what the hell he had meant by the remark. Billy had intended going home to wash and change before meeting Suzy, but after a pint or two he had become too lazy and had stayed put. He told himself he would go after his third pint.

As Jonny hoped, Billy was propping up the bar in the Passage pub. He usually popped in for a swift pint or two after work especially on Friday's, even if he was meeting Suzy. Jonny tapped Billy on the shoulder. He turned and tensed when he saw it was Jonny. Would the stuck up bitch Sarah have grassed him up about their earlier conversation?

It was all right. Jonny was smiling pleasantly. "Hi Billy, I'm glad I've found you. I've got something for you" Billy grinned in anticipation. Maybe he was going to cough up some dosh after all.

"What you got for me, then, Jon?" he slurred, looking at Jonny expectantly. He had stayed longer in the pub than he should have. He was feeling pissed all ready.

Jonny punched Billy as hard as he could, turned on his heel without another word, and left.

Suzy had thought long and hard about what to do. She was not going to tell Billy, for a start. She had tentatively broached the subject with him of children to test the waters as it were, after telling Sarah that she had been stupid enough to get herself up the duff. She could not quite believe her own bad luck. She thought she was safe as she had been on the pill for a couple of years now. She had been so sick with a hangover the night of Jonny's dad's party; it must have stopped it working. She could not get over Billy's face when she had brought up the subject of children. He had been appalled, saying that he wasn't cut out to be a father, not now or ever, and he hoped she wasn't getting broody. No bird is ever gonna trap me, he had said. She had laughed, and said no, of course not, even though it had cut her to the quick.

Then he had really broken her heart. He had had a lot to drink of course, but Suzy was still mortified when he had slurred at her and said, "Anyway, Suze, I know what a little goer you are! You're the good time that was had by all, ain't yer? If you ever got up the duff, I'd never know if it was mine or not! You must've had more pricks than a second hand dart board! Hahahaha!!"

Suzy had sobbed alone in her bedroom after that. Any last lingering feeling's she might have had for Billy had evaporated. What a right charmer he was! She wondered what she had ever seen in him. Oh, he was good looking, and he could turn on the charm when he wanted to, but once you got to know him he had about as much appeal as a porcupine with halitosis. She made her mind up to give him the elbow. She would tell him when he had sobered up, hopefully on their next date. She had been so upset when he had called her a good time girl that she had left the pub they had been drinking in without another word. Billy had not come after her. He had waited for over a week before ringing her. She had agreed to meet him at the Golden Hind pub on Friday. She was determined to finish things. She felt much better now she had made her decision. She also decided that the only thing, the best thing, she could do was to have a termination. She knew it would cost a hell of a lot of money, but although she did not have much in the way of savings, she did have premium bonds that her mum and dad bought her every year for Christmas. None of her numbers had ever bloody come up, and they were only sitting there in her dressing table drawer. She would cash them in, and get herself out of trouble. She wiped her eyes, and felt a bit better.

Suzy had seen her doctor, and cashed in her premium bonds. She had enough money to pay for the termination, and to treat herself to something nice to cheer herself up after. She had had to see two doctors, and be lectured about the error of her ways. She had had to talk about why it would be worse for her to have this baby than not have it. It had been excruciating, and she had

124

longed for the whole ordeal to be over. The money was tucked away in her purse, and the procedure was all booked for Monday morning. Her parents knew nothing about it, but Sarah had been bloody brilliant, and had promised to go with her. She had not seen sight nor sound of Billy since his charming speech, but he had asked her to go for a drink, and they were meeting tonight. She was going to dump him, and could not wait. The more she thought about the way he had treated her, the angrier she had become.

It had been horrible telling Billy, much worse than she had imagined. Billy was already half cut when Suzy had met him outside the Golden Hind Pub. He must have been drinking for quite a while, because he already looked pissed. He was still in his greasy work clothes too. He could have made a bit of an effort, Suzy told herself crossly. "What happened to your eye?" Suzy said suspiciously. It was black and blue.

"I had a little accident… at work," Billy slurred. Suzy sighed. He sounded very pissed indeed. This was going to be a lot harder than she had anticipated. It was crowded inside, and hardly conducive to a private conversation. Suzy wondered how long he had been there before she arrived. He looked pissed as a newt. In the end, Suzy had asked if they could go back to her flat, her parents had gone out, and her brother Robert was at his mates house, and she had something to tell him. She was beginning to wish she had taken the coward's way out and told him it was over by phone. Looking at him now, she felt she did not owe him a face-to-face confrontation. Still, it was too late to back out now.

He had thought it was a perfect excuse to have sex, and had almost dragged her into her bedroom as soon as the front door had closed. He was always amorous when he was pissed. The walk to her house from the pub had done little to sober him up. His amorous antics had become a real turn off, too. He had tried to grope her as they walked along the street. People had starred. She had made excuses, and gone to the toilet to compose herself as soon as she had wrestled away from his clutches.

Suzy took deep breaths before coming out and gently asking him to sit with her in the living room. He had looked disappointed, expecting her to reappear wearing some sexy undies. He got off her bed reluctantly. Suzy looked irritated. She was losing her patience, and keen for Billy to leave. "I'm not some bloody sex doll that you can dress up whenever you want to get your leg over!" Suzy had told him furiously. He had gone all sulky when he saw she was still fully clothed, and looked quite astonished by her out- burst, but he had followed her into the living room reluctantly.

Once he had parked himself on the leatherette couch, she had taken a deep breath, and told him it was over. He had actually laughed, and tried to kiss her. When she had pushed him away, he had turned nasty, calling her a stupid little slag. He lunged forward again, breathing his beery breath all over her. His black eye was by now swollen and discoloured, and made Suzy feel queasy. In fact, she felt quite revolted being near him. He reeked of booze and engine oil and she had to swallow hard to fight down the nausea that was rising in her throat. She had tried her best to be calm, and told him again she didn't think they should see each other anymore. He had looked at her in disbelief, the arrogant little git. Sitting in her parent's living room, he had sworn at her viciously. Then he had said good riddance, he would be better off without her, slags like her were ten a penny, and had jumped up and slammed out of the flat. Suzy hurriedly put the chain on the front door the moment it slammed shut.

Tearfully, she had made herself a cup of tea to try to calm herself down. She was shaking. She had not expected him to be pleased, but she was still shocked at how nasty he had been. She told herself she had had a lucky escape, and took her steaming cup of tea into her bedroom. She wondered if Sarah would be at home, and decided to ring her. Just as she went to pick up the phone, it rang. When Suzy answered it, it was Sarah. "Great minds think alike! I was just about to ring you..."

Suzy was shocked when Sarah told her she too had had a row with Billy. She had been so upset Jonny had taken her home early. As the whole sordid story unfolded, Suzy realised exactly what a narrow escape she had had. When she had told Sarah about her own evening with Billy the charmer, Sarah agreed with her. Sarah was relieved that Suzy had finally come to her senses and told Billy to piss off. The two girls chatted for ages, and both finally ended up feeling much better. Suzy eventually said her ears were sore, they had been talking so long. They laughed and said their goodbyes.

It was not until Suzy had taken her make up off, and went to get her nightie out of her drawer that she noticed her purse open and empty on the floor near her bed. All her premium bond money was gone.

Billy had only looked in the drawer to be nosy. He half hoped there might be a Durex in there. He hoped he would get lucky tonight. Why else would good old Suzy invite him to her flat? She was on the pill, or so she said, but she had started hinting about kids, and he didn't want to take any chances. He wouldn't put it past her to try and trick him. He had decided not to ride her bare back anymore. He hadn't been able to believe his luck when he spotted her purse. He had thought she might have stashed away the odd fiver, maybe, but when he had found it crammed with money, his eyes had nearly popped out of his head! Maybe it wasn't such a bad life, after all.

Billy had turned into Packington Street, whistling happily. He had a wallet full of cash and he was free as a bird again. Tomorrow, he told himself, he would be out on the pull again.

"Hello, Billy boy"

Billy felt his blood freeze in his veins.

It was Nick Crowley. Billy's mouth had gone suddenly dry. "You better have something for me, Billy boy, or I'm afraid you will be singing soprano instead of whistling very soon"

Billy fumbled in his jacket pocket and pulled out Suzy's money. Thank God, he had it. It was not quite enough to pay off Nick, but it was not far off. "Here...here you are, Nick, mate. I...I. got this for you...it's not all of it, I know, but...I will get the rest, I promise..." he was sweating now, and licked his lips nervously.

Nick was silent, and counted out the notes Billy had nervously handed him. Billy saw two of Nick Crowley's henchmen standing further up the street. He knew them well. He had seen them a few years ago knife a poor sap outside a pub. The poor geezer had owed Nick money. The man, just twenty years old, had bled to death on the pavement. Billy felt his knees begin to buckle, and he tried hard to compose himself. Nick Crowley allowed himself a smile. A shark's smile. He observed Billy's swollen eye, but remained silent. Billy swallowed hard. Finally, Nick said,

"Very good, Billy boy, but it's just a drop in the Ocean, my friend. You know, it's a good thing I'm a very patient man. I would hate to think you are trying to take the piss, little Billy boy. I don't like it when people take the piss. I tell you what. I'll give you til next Friday. Then I want the rest. All of it, you understand?"

He grabbed Billy's face with his large ring filled fingers. "Yes, I can see you understand, Billy boy. Don't forget the interest, mind. I want £500 now." Billy went white. £500? He only owed £100 to begin with! Where was he going to get that amount from in a week?

" You had better not be late, Billy boy. I hate it when people keep me waiting. It would be such a shame….and if you haven't got the money by then, well, you won't be seeing me anymore…" Billy looked puzzled.

"Why…why won't I see you, Mr Crowley?" Billy whispered. It was hard to speak louder, as Nick Crowley still had his face squeezed between his fingers. "You won't be seeing me, or anyone else, come to think of it, cos if I don't get my money, I'm gonna poke your fucking eyes out…"

Suzy's mum and dad, Joycie and Bob, found Suzy sobbing her heart out when they came home from visiting Joycie's sister. Suzy had become hysterical, and had not wanted to talk at first, but Joycie had said firmly that Suzy had better tell her, and looked so worried, that the whole sorry story had come out. Suzy had expected her dad, especially, to go ballistic. He did, but not because Suzy was pregnant. He had been Suzy had to admit, quite magnificent. He had said he would find the no good randy little bastard that had got his girl into trouble and rip his bollocks off with pliers and let Suzy use them as earrings. He had sworn a lot when Suzy tearfully confessed that she had cashed in her premium bonds, and that Billy had nicked all of the money. He told her she was a stupid cow, but then, unexpectedly, he had put his arms around her, and hugged her to him. Suzy had sobbed again then, all over her dad's new and hideous beige safari suit. "Don't you worry, Angel" he told her, his voice choked, "Don't you worry about anyfink. Yer ole dad'll sort it. It's all gonna be fine, darlin"

Billy shakily took his door keys out of his pocket as he stepped out of the lift. It was only 10.30pm on a Friday night, but already the lift smelled of piss. The drunks had been busy already. God, he hated this poxy estate. He wanted better things. He swallowed hard, wrinkled his nose in disgust and tried not to inhale. As he went to put his key into the lock, he noticed the new keys on his key ring. They were a spare set of keys to Jonny's house.

Victor Mason had had the locks changed after the little slag Louise had nicked Jonny's keys that time. Billy had helpfully volunteered to get them cut for him. He had a set cut for himself, thinking they might come in handy one day. He grinned, and turned the key in his own front door. He had to get a few things ready first, but... That day had just come.

Victor Mason strolled along Duncan Terrace and let Truffle bumble his way to the house whilst he fumbled in his jacket pocket for his door keys. He had taken Truffle for an evening walk along the canal. Jonny and Sarah had gone out for the evening, and he had been bored sitting indoors on his own. There was nothing worth watching on television and he had just finished reading a good book. He was so relieved that the two of them had made up after their ridiculous row. Billy had a lot to answer for.

He had phoned Jonny from his hotel room after that fruitless auction and Jon had been absolutely distraught. He had refused to tell him what was wrong at first, but then the whole sorry story had come tumbling out in a rush. Bloody Louise! Victor would make sure her father heard what the conniving little minx had been up to! He was certainly going to have a few words with Billy too, the vindictive little swine. What did he think he was playing at, putting those photos in Jonny's drawer instead of throwing them away! That was just plain nasty. He could not see how their friendship could be salvaged after that. It was a shame, but Jonny was better off without him. Victor whistled to Truffle as he sniffed at a lamppost and the dog wagged his tail in acknowledgement, and carried on sniffing. Victor smiled fondly at his dog and fished his door keys out of his pocket.

As he reached his doorstep, he was surprised to see that the front door was open. He knew he had carefully locked it on his way out. Cautiously he pushed it and walked quietly inside. The front door had not been forced, but he knew Jonny and Sarah would not be home yet, and would never leave the front door open like this, even if they had come home unexpectedly early. Truffle, as usual, made straight for his water bowl in the kitchen. They both heard movement from upstairs, and Truffle let out a loud startled bark. "Who's there?" Victor called out. Cautiously, he climbed the stairs.

A figure dressed in black wearing a balaclava came out of Jonny's bedroom.

Victor Mason felt his heart pumping but he raced up the stairs and rugby tackled the intruder. The pair crashed to the floor and rolled struggling on the landing. Victor older but heavier than the intruder, managed to gain the upper hand, and sat astride the man, who was still struggling to escape. Using his knees to pin his arms down, Victor pulled off the struggling man's balaclava.

It was Billy.

Victor was so shocked, he released his grip on Billy's legs momentarily and Billy, seizing his advantage, sat up with a jerk, pitching Victor backwards. Quickly Billy was on his feet. Victor was panting, but managed to say quietly "My God, Billy, what the hell are you doing? Why would you steal from us?" he was still reeling from shock. How could one of Jonny's friends do something like this? They had both trusted him implicitly. Billy had dropped a large holdall on the floor when Victor tackled him, which was no doubt filled with all the belongings he and Jonny had worked so hard for. Victor was furious, and began to get up.

From his jacket pocket, Billy had produced a large kitchen knife. Victor recognised it as one from a set in Jonny's kitchen. "Don't be so bloody stupid!" Victor said angrily, as Billy edged forward brandishing the knife.

They were the last words Victor Mason said.

CHAPTER FIVE

It had all gone wrong. Billy held his head in his hands, and stood over the slumped body of Victor Mason. Blood was oozing from the knife wounds in his chest and he lay unconscious at his feet. Billy could hear the stupid fucking dog barking his head off, and felt panic rising like bile in his throat. Why had he stabbed him more than once? The first thrust of the knife had been pure instinct, lashing out to save his own miserable skin, but the others... as Victor's eyes had closed and he lost consciousness, Billy could hear a voice inside of his head urging him on. Victor couldn't tell the filth it was him, he couldn't go to prison. So he had plunged the knife into Victor again and again.

Finally, he looked down at his blood-spattered jacket and realised the enormity of what he had done. He was shaking now, his heart was booming and he was sweating profusely. All his instincts told him to run. He looked round frantically for the holdall he had brought. He picked it up and tried to take deep breaths to calm himself down. He used the back of his hand to wipe the beads of sweat away from his forehead. He panicked, wondering if he had smeared blood onto his own face. There was so much blood. He still had the blood stained knife in his hand, and hastily, he shoved it into the holdall. Don't run, don't run he told himself, still doing his deep breathing. Don't draw attention to yourself. He went into Jonny's tiny bathroom and looked at his reflection. Why wouldn't that dog shut the fuck up? He splashed water onto his face to calm himself, and remove any traces of Victor's blood. He cleaned the sink making sure not to leave any fingerprints on anything. His jacket had blood on it, but the jacket was black, so no one would notice unless they got up close to him. He hoped not, anyway. He tried to talk calmly to himself. Walk casually out of the house, close the door quietly behind you. Walk normally down the street. Cross over by ColeBrooke Row. Go and sit down by the canal and gather your thoughts. He recited the advice to himself repeatedly in his head.

He averted his eyes from Victor Mason, and gripping the handles of the holdall firmly, he walked downstairs. Victor had left his wallet and door keys on the hall table. Billy picked up the wallet, walked past the still barking dog and out of the front door.

Sitting on a bench by the side of the Regents canal, Billy worked out a plan. He knew he could not go home. He had to make a run for it, but where could he go? He didn't have a passport, so going abroad was out. Besides, he was afraid the cops would be checking. He was sure he had killed poor bloody Victor Mason. He was terrified. Robbery was bad enough, but he couldn't do time for murder! No, he had to get away, somewhere they would never thing of looking for him, and somewhere not even Nick Crowley would think of.

Slowly, an idea came to him, and despite himself, he could not help grinning. That's it! He told himself, a eureka moment. His mum had received a postcard from her pal Gwen this morning. She was on holiday on the Isle of Wight. Billy had only ever been there once, as a little kid, but he had been to the Reading Rock festival in 1976 and met a girl there from The Isle of Wight.

Nina something or other, he had a brief fling with her. She had been all over Billy like a rash. She was older than Billy, not bad looking, but with a great pair of knockers. He knew she lived in

Shanklin, on the Isle of Wight, and she worked as a receptionist for a big hotel. He could find her. She would be his ticket out of this mess.

She would fall for his charms he knew it. He could sweet talk any bird if he put his mind to it. He could sweet talk just about anyone, come to think of it. He was an expert at manipulating people he told himself confidently. He had managed to get Jonny eating out of the palm of his hand with no trouble at all. He had listened to the conversations in the garage before he even met Jonny. Victor had told his boss George all about his son, and how he was at university. He had spoken of his son with such pride in his voice. Billy had been jealous of Jonny long before they had even met.

All Billy had had to do when they did meet was feign interest in the things he already knew Jonny liked, and that was that, he had made a friend. He had always been able to get round his own mother in the same way. She had always fallen for it. The old girl thought he was the apple of her eye.

He took out Victor's wallet. He looked through it carefully. There was over twenty quid in it. It was enough for now. He picked up the holdall and walked as casually as he could to find a car. Stealing one was easy when you knew how.

Nina Taylor had hardly been able to believe her eyes. She had looked up from her desk straight into the very brown eyes of Billy Jameson! There he was, grinning down at her, just as gorgeous as she remembered him from last year's Reading Rock festival. Their eyes had met across a crowded beer stand. He had given her the same grin he was giving her now. He had said he was only going to stay for the day, he was fed up with the rain, the can fights and the racist taunts every time a reggae act came on stage, and he had managed to lose his mates in the crowd.

Somehow, he had ended up staying for the whole weekend. Nina's friends did not seem to mind her going off with Billy. Nina had happily led Billy off to listen to the roaring music and from that moment on, they had stayed together all the time, dancing in the crowd together, singing along to Eddie and the Hot Rods, shouting at the top of their lungs "Do anything you wanna do" then kissing as their feet had got stuck in the mud.

They had laughed at the irony, 1976 had seen Britain in the grip of a bloody heat wave, it had been the hottest summer for decades, but of course, it was an unwritten rule, it had to rain at a rock festival.

Despite the rain and a leaky shared tent, they had had the most amazing sex she had ever had in her life. While her friends went off to listen to the music, she and Billy had made their own kind of music inside the tent.

Nina had been very tearful when their time together had ended. They both promised to keep in touch, but Nina felt in her heart that she was only kidding herself. She had sent him the odd postcard when he went home, but did not think she would ever meet up with him again. She had her memories, and tried to be philosophical about it. Now, here he was, standing right in front of her. She tried to remain calm, but could not keep the delighted look off her face as she asked him what he was doing here.

1979

It had all gone much better than he had expected. Billy felt quite pleased with himself. When he had finally stepped off the ferry he had had a moment of doubt, but Nina had been quite easy to find. He knew she worked for the biggest hotel on the Isle of Wight, and he had gone into a tourist board office and asked a few questions. He had sold some of the stuff he had nicked from the robbery in a little antique shop he had found. He used the money as a deposit and rented a small bedsit for the time being, and had even got himself a job as a barman. It was a poxy job, the pay was absolute crap, but it would do until he could find something better, maybe in a garage somewhere. He was a good mechanic, and was confident he would find somewhere he could prove how good he was. He could not afford to be choosy yet, so he had accepted the first job on offer.

He had spun Nina a load of old flannel, telling her he hadn't been able to get her out of his head since he met her, but said he had lost her address, and had come to look for her the first chance he had got. She looked incredulous at first, and he thought he had blown it by going too far, but he had turned up where she worked every day, with flowers, and chocolates, and plenty more sweet talk until he wore her down. He had taken her out to dinner, bought her presents and listened as she droned on endlessly about her job in the hotel. He had laughed in all the right places, got outraged on her behalf when she whined about her ugly male chauvinist boss, and he knew that she had fallen for him. He could see it in her eyes.

Now, here he was, two years later, living in her modest but immaculate flat, working in a garage earning a decent wage at last. He had stopped looking over his shoulder all the time waiting for the filth to arrest him. At first, he had scoured the newspapers, and watched the news on telly, waiting for reports about a robbery and murder in London. As the weeks passed, and the weeks turned into months and he had not heard a thing about it, he began to relax. He had been relieved to leave the pub job, but even that had had unexpected bonuses.

He had met Michael Harper, known by all the regulars as Mucky Micky whilst he worked as a barman in The Coach and Horses public House. Old Mucky was a regular customer himself, and he came in most nights. Mucky was a weaselly looking man, with thin greying hair who ran an illegal sex shop above a grubby little office. He also made porn films, and told the pub regulars all about them when the bar manager was out of earshot.

Paul Brennan, the bar manager wasn't stupid, he knew only too well what line of business Mucky Micky was in, but he chose to turn a blind eye. Mucky Micky liked a drink, and he spent many hours and many fivers in the pub. It did not do to upset any of the regulars, and quite a few extra punters turned up regularly to sample whatever Mucky had on offer.

Mucky Mickey had film nights in his grubby little shop after the pubs shut every Friday night. Billy had been very interested when Mucky Micky had said he was always on the lookout for girls to be in his grubby little home movies. Mucky had a thriving business making his porn films in seedy little bedsits all over the Isle of Wight, and had recently branched out on the main land. He joked that all the nasty padded headboards on the Isle of Wight were featured in his blue movies, and he hoped there would be many more from the main land.

Billy had a bit of a windfall soon after making the acquaintance of Mucky. One of his Gee Gee's had romped home at 50 to 1. He had talked it over with Mucky, and had bought a discreet cine camera from him. It was very easy to set up at home, Mucky had said, and had showed him how to operate it.

One day when Nina was working a late shift at the hotel, Billy had installed it on a bookshelf in the bedroom. It was an expensive bit of kit, and Billy knew that Nina would not know it was there. Billy had surprised Nina by building the bookcase for her. He had made a big deal out of telling her he wanted to make something special for her. He told her he knew she loved her books, and said he would make her a set of shelves so she didn't have to keep them in cardboard boxes shut up in the wardrobe anymore. As he had hoped, she had been absolutely delighted. Billy had set to work and he had made a secret panel in which to hide the camera. It was very well hidden. He stood back and admired his own handy work. He knew all those poxy woodwork lessons at school would come in handy one day. He grinned to himself, and ran his fingers over the smooth pine shelving.

Nina had been thrilled with the bookshelf, and had arranged all her books lovingly on them as soon as Billy had put away his screwdriver. She had thought herself very lucky to have such a handy man for a boyfriend.

Billy started buying Nina all sorts of sexy outfits and underwear, and at first, she was thrilled. She had been so pleased with her bookshelves that she had laughingly said she would have to find a way to thank him for his trouble. He had leered naughtily at her, and said, "I'm sure you will repay me, darling" and he had taken her straight to bed. Their sex life had always been good, but now, Billy had become insatiable. Since he had started to buy her all the raunchy outfits, he liked to wear a mask when they did it that totally obscured his own face. Nina didn't like it, it gave her the creeps. She had asked him once or twice to take the mask off, as she wanted him to kiss her, but he always said no. He said it really turned him on when he wore it, so Nina had so far put up with it. He got her to do some pretty kinky things in the bedroom now, and it had stopped being fun. Nina was beginning to dread going home.

When they first got together, sex had been exciting, but had always been loving, too. Billy had always held her afterwards, and given her kisses and cuddles. Now, Nina felt that it was becoming a bit seedy and she was beginning to feel used and taken for granted. Billy had turned from a lover into a selfish oaf who was only interested in his own gratification. It was wham, bam, thank you ma'am time. He always wanted her to dress up for sex. They never made love anymore it was just sex. He had bought her a nurse's outfit, then a naughty nun's outfit, and then some black PVC underwear. Every week he would turn up with something new, and he would tell her she looked incredibly sexy in everything she put on. At first, she had been flattered, and had been eager to please him, but now as the outfits got more and more bizarre, she just felt ridiculous, and she was not always happy doing the things that Billy wanted. As time went on he asked her to do some quite horrible and painful acts, but he was always incredibly appreciative afterwards, and so Nina went along with it. She had always believed that the way to keep a man was to keep him happy in bed. She realised that she had fallen in love with Billy, and she wanted to make him happy. She just wished that now and again he would try to make her happy too. In the last few months, he had taken it for granted that she would go along with whatever he demanded she do, and her eagerness to please was beginning to wear out. She loved him, but she was starting to become somewhat disenchanted with her life.

Billy was earning a small fortune from the very explicit recordings   that he took to Mucky Micky's shop. In a matter of weeks, Naughty Nina's naked adventures were being viewed by dirty old men all over the Island, and far and wide on the mainland too. Mucky Micky was delighted, and so was Billy. Mucky Mickey had told Billy that he was about to do a deal with a sex shop in London's Soho, and that would really rake in the money.

Nina had been having a quiet drink after work with her friend, Lucy. Billy was working late tonight. A group of men kept giving her funny looks. It wasn't her imagination, she was sure of it. They kept looking over at her, nudging one another and smirking. When Nina went to get another drink, one of the men shouted out to her "Oi Oi it's, Naughty Nina! Hello, darling!" Nina felt herself blushing. The vile man was actually blowing her kisses. How the hell did he know her name anyway and what the hell was he jabbering about? She tried to ignore him, but he stood up and lurched over. "Come on, Nina, don't go all coy on me. You're not coy in your blue movies, are you darling?"

CHAPTER SIX

Eleanor Parish took her first holiday alone in the summer of
1979. It had become very fashionable to go on holiday in
America, and Eleanor was keen to spread her wings for once in
her life and go on an adventure. She had begun to feel that life
was passing her by. She was achingly lonely and had always
been afraid of holidaying alone. After hearing yet another
rapturous tale in the executive dining room about the wonders
of California, her mind was made up. Before she could talk
herself out of it, she took herself off to the travel agent during
her lunch break and booked her trip.

She had planned to hire a car and travel around California. She
wanted to start in San Francisco and go where her mood took
her. She chose not to drive in Central London as parking was
such a nightmare but she thought it might be fun to drive along
Route 66. Besides, she didn't much fancy going on a Greyhound
bus with a bunch of complete strangers all feeling sorry for her
because she was traveling on her own.

It was on her first evening that she met Martha in a little bar by
Fisherman's Wharf, on pier 39. Martha had served her with a
smile and said in a thick southern drawl "You all alone, Sugar?"
Eleanor had smiled, and raised her glass before saying shyly
"Indeed I am, but that's fine. I like it that way"

"The hell you do!" Martha had replied with a smile. She had
poured herself a drink and had come over for a chat. Before
Eleanor realised it, the evening had passed pleasantly away and

the night outside was very dark. Eleanor wondered idly how the hell she was going to find her way back to her hotel. Martha had loved Eleanor's English accent, and had asked her if she had a place to stay. She looked aghast when Eleanor had said she had booked into a small hotel called The Golden Gate. Eleanor had left her hired car in the hotel car park and she had walked to the bar to explore. She could not remember the way back to the car park.

"Sugar, you ain't gonna like it there. They got cockroaches bigger than buffaloes an I don't s'pose they change their sheets more'n once every Thanksgiving. Honey, you more'n welcome to stay with me. I got a nice lil apartment above the bar. Not far to stagger home to, an if you don't like it, you can always change your mind an go off to The Bates Motel. That's what we call the Golden Gate anyways. Be sure to say hi to Norman for me." She winked wickedly and poured herself another drink. She had been drinking cocktails all night and her glass was as big as a gold fish bowl.

Eleanor had seen the film Pyscho, and didn't much fancy snuggling up to Norman Bates or a Buffalo sized cockroach. She had had far more to drink than she intended, and could no longer feel her legs. She only intended to go and take a look at Martha's apartment out of curiosity. She was sure there must be a better hotel close by. Surely, she could go and collect her things and sort it out without too much difficulty.

She ended up staying with Martha for three weeks. It had been the best three weeks she had ever had in her life.

Martha taught Eleanor not to be afraid of who she was. She had roared with laughter at Eleanor's look of shocked surprise when she had seen an openly gay couple of men driving along in an open top car wearing nail varnish and make up. "Bet you don't see anything like that in the pea souper's in London, ah sugar?"

"Pea souper's?" Eleanor had said laughing, "It's not Victorian times in London you know! We haven't seen a pea souper fog since Jack the Ripper!"

By the time Eleanor had to say goodbye to Martha, she knew that she would never be the same again. She kissed Martha goodbye and hugged her close. She wasn't unhappy, she had never felt so alive in her entire life and she knew she would always be eternally grateful to Martha. When she went back to work, she had a new spring in her step and even the Pan Stick people noticed the change in her.

In September she enrolled for an evening class in pottery. She had been inspired by the little artist studios she had seen in San Francisco and decided to have a go herself at something creative. She smiled to herself, and thought Martha would be proud of her. She didn't discover an untapped talent at the potter's wheel. She did, however meet the love of her life. By Christmas, she and Catherine her pottery class teacher had moved in together and by the following spring, Catherine had converted Eleanor's shed into a pottery studio and had settled in very well.

Carrie Miller sat on the floor of her living room with her back to the wall. She slumped forward, hugging her legs for comfort with her chin on her knees. She was not sure how long she had been there, but it had grown dark. The shadows had been comforting, somehow. Carrie felt as if they had thrown a protective blanket around her, hiding her eyes, shielding her from the terrible thing she had done.

She had been hysterical at first, and had sobbed uncontrollably, apologising to the still warm body of her husband lying on the couch. Then she began to get angry. With herself at first, but then at Tommy. "You were never sorry, were you?" she said coldly, in a harsh little whisper. Her voice, ragged and full of emotion cut through the silent air like a switchblade. She wiped the tears from her face roughly with the back of her hand, and sniffed loudly. "All these years, Tom, all these years... and all those good hidings you gave me...not once...oh Tom, not once did you ever say sorry! You always made me feel like it was my own fault! Like I was the one in the wrong!" Her voice broke, and she let out a sob before saying quietly, "Oh Tom...Tom...I loved you so! I'm sorry Tommy, I'm so so sorry..."

Carrie was not afraid. She was prepared to face the consequences of her actions if need be. She reasoned with herself that even if she had to go to prison, it could not be any worse than the fear she had felt in her own home all these years. She did not want to leave Sarah, of course, but she had reached the end of her tether. She had tried so hard since Tommy had come home from the hospital. She had convinced herself it would be different this time. She told herself that she would get her old Tommy back, the Tommy she had fallen in love with all those years ago. The Tommy she loved. He had been stuck in that hospital ward for so long, and he had changed. All the staff there had said what a lovely man he was, helpful, polite, and eager to get better and go home.

At first, it really had been okay. Carrie thought she saw a glimpse of the Tommy she used to love, the Tommy who had courted her as a young innocent schoolgirl, the Tommy who had held her in the darkness of the night and whispered to her between kisses. She ached for him. She was so lonely without him. The man he had become over the years was cruel and vicious. He had become an alcoholic thug. She admitted to herself now that she was terrified of him, and each day filled her with dread. It was like living with a ticking time bomb never knowing if or when he would explode. She was never afraid of the reign of terror gripping London from the I.R.A who had planted bombs all over the city, for being at home was so much more terrifying for her.

Carrie had tasted a different way of life while he had been away. He had been in the rehabilitation hospital for a whole year. She had enjoyed her bit of independence. She had even found herself a nice little job, in an office, and had made friends there. She had a regular weekly wage and had opened a little savings account for herself. She had even started going out once a week, to Bingo with Joycie. Life was good. She could not go back, not now she had seen how carefree life could be.

Tommy had wanted to put a stop to it all, of course. He had said she had better give up her job when he got home. He needed her at home to look after him. He was an invalid and Carrie would have to be his full time carer. He had been furious when she said she couldn't do that, they needed the money. He had been furious, but had grudgingly admitted that the money had come in handy so he had given in and let her keep on working.

Although he would never be as fit as he was before the stroke, he was perfectly capable of managing by himself. His speech was not clear, but he could communicate. His mouth was still fixed in an odd grimace, but it had improved a great deal. He had difficulty doing everyday tasks, but he could do them if he took his time. The hospital staff had done an excellent job, and he had made very good progress. Tommy however, liked to be pandered to. Carrie had to wait on him hand and foot when she was at home, and she was beginning to get exhausted. He made her help him in and out of bed, and he was heavy. He made her help him get washed, get dressed. He even made her help him go to the toilet. She knew he was capable of doing most things on his own, but he liked her being at his disposal. It was just another of his little power trips. Carrie was grimly aware of what he was up to, but found herself once again too afraid to refuse.

For the first few weeks, he had been grateful, and said often that it was good to be home. He had not had a drink since coming home, and although she was exhausted, Carrie was coping. Sarah had been a tower of strength. She always helped when she was home, and Jonny would help too, by giving her a lift to get groceries. Tommy behaved himself when Sarah and Jonny were around.

When the novelty of being back in familiar surroundings began to wear off, Tommy began to be short tempered. He complained that Carrie had not cooked his dinner the way he liked it, that he was bored, that he didn't like Sarah spending so much time with Jonny. Carrie felt her nerves begin to jangle in the old familiar way. She fought down the panic inside her, and tried to placate him. Her newfound confidence was beginning to slip once again, like dirty bath water down a plughole. She was resentful. She began to make stupid mistakes at work and got flustered and tearful. It was not bloody fair, she told herself. She didn't know what she had ever done to deserve it.

She couldn't quite put her finger on what had set him off this time. Over the last two weeks, he had started to get more and more abusive and all the old fears had begun to rise to the surface for Carrie. Tommy was becoming bored and frustrated.

He wanted a drink. He was capable of being much more independent than he let on, but he enjoyed Carrie being around to attend his every need. He still got her to do everything for him. He had shouted and sworn at Carrie, because she had refused to have any alcohol in the house. Tommy was not strong enough yet to leave the house on his own. He refused to use the stick he had been given to help support him, saying it made him look like an old man. He would not use a wheel chair either. Carrie knew it would not be too long before he would give in as he hated being cooped up indoors, and the thought of him going out to the pub and coming home pissed filled her with dread.

Carrie found herself becoming easily flustered at home as well as at work, and she dropped a cup in front of Tommy. He had been watching her make a cup of tea intently and as she felt his eyes boring into her, she felt herself tremble. The cup had rattled in her grasp, and fallen with a crash and a clatter onto the hard kitchen tiles. Tommy had called her a clumsy bitch, and as she walked past him, to find the dustpan and brush, Tommy had pinched her arm. She jerked away, as if scolded. She had been surprised at how quickly he had been able to lash out. "Don't you dare!" she blurted out, without thinking, rubbing her sore arm. Tommy looked shocked. She had never answered back before. "What did you say?" he said slowly and quietly, menacingly.

Carrie felt her heart race. She tried to be brave. She licked her lips and swallowed hard before saying in a tremulous little voice "I...I'm not..going to put up with your bullying anymore, Tom. Not anymore. ..I won't have it!" she tried to sound assertive, but her knees were beginning to buckle. "And I'm not going to wait on you hand and foot anymore either! It..it's not good for you. You need to be independent! The doctor's said so.." Her voice trailed off and her eyes widened in terror as Tommy stood up slowly. So, he could walk when he wanted to, she thought as she swallowed hard again.

He did not say anything until he reached Carrie. He was still a little weak down his left side, but he could move remarkably swiftly when he put his mind to it. His mouth was still a little twisted, and as he loomed over Carrie, his expression became a terrifying grimace. He reached out his right arm and grabbed Carries hair, pulling hard and forcing her head back. He put his twisted face inches from her eyes and said through gritted teeth, "You will do as I fucking say, and don't you ever answer me back again" He gave her a vicious shove and she fell to the floor.

It was in that moment that realisation finally dawned on Carrie. Her nightmare would never be over as long as Tommy lived.

Tommy always insisted on doing his own insulin injections. The district nurse had done a home visit after he had come home from hospital, and been quite impressed at his level of independence, especially regarding his medication. He had put on a good show for the nurse. He had dismissed her offer of help, and said curtly that he was quite capable, thank you very much. He had given her a "don't teach your grandmother to suck eggs" look when she had tried to advise him about rotating the sites of his injections, in order to avoid infection, or pooling of insulin under the skin, like he hadn't heard the same old garbage a million times before. He had been giving himself his insulin for fucking years; he did not need some interfering old cow telling him what to do. He would not allow Carrie to do it for him, either. He did not want anyone else sticking needles into his flesh. He was relieved when the old witch had gone, and left him in peace to read his Daily Mirror.

Carrie had waited until he fell asleep on the couch that evening. He was drunk, of course. He had insisted she go out to buy him his cans of beer. She had not wanted to, and had refused at first, but he had thrown his mug of hot tea she had made him across the room at her and threatened to cave her fucking head in. She already had a livid bruise on her arm from where he had pinched her. Some of the hot tea had splashed on her arm and she felt the sting of the hot liquid as it ran down her already bruised arm.

Luckily for her, his friend, Frank Gloucester from the brewery had popped round just after she had cleared up the mess from the tea. Frank had brought two Party 7 cans with him, so she did not have to go out for him after all. She could honestly say to the police that she had not brought alcohol into the house, if they ever asked her. Frank was just about the only friend that Tommy had not alienated with his drinking. They had known each other since their army days during the war and they had worked together at the brewery but Carrie had never liked Frank. He was a sharp featured little man and he made Carrie feel very uncomfortable. She was happy to leave the two of them alone whilst she scuttled off to the safety of her bedroom.

Tommy had fallen asleep and was snoring loudly. He had forgotten to have his insulin. He had got himself so drunk, drinking almost all of the beer that Frank had brought; that he had passed out just after Frank had staggered off home.

Carrie had hidden herself away in the bedroom when Frank had arrived and stayed there. She knew she would be surplus to requirements. Tommy would summon her as if she was the ruddy maid service if he wanted anything. She tried to settle herself down with her library book, but she couldn't concentrate. She knew that the more Tommy drank, the more obnoxious he would become. She lay on her bed and listened to the muffled conversation through the walls.

As the day wore on, she had heard Tommy getting maudlin with Frank. Through the paper-thin walls of the flat, she heard Tommy bemoan about his ruddy life, and what a hard time he had had. His voice began to rise in the whinny self-pitying way that was so familiar to Carrie. He always felt sorry for himself when his belly was full of beer. "I sometimes wonder if it's all worth it!" she heard him slur loudly, and then he said, "What've I got to show for all my years of hard work? Fuck all, Frank! Not a fucking fing! I won't ever be able to go back to work. Look at me, I'm a useless cripple! Sometimes fink I'd've been better orf if I hadn't survived that poxy 'orse kickin me! It would've bin a mercy killing Frank! I fink I should've topped me self, like poofy Walter did..." he began to snivel. Carrie heard Frank say in a soft wheedling tone "There now Tom. Don't go getting all choked up. Walter was a poor little sod.. just a kid, he was what, eighteen? We should nevver 'ave tormented 'im like we did, but we were'nt to know he'd go an' do a fing like that....'ave a nuvver drink, mate. I still fink of 'im, you know..Walter, I mean. We didn't mean it, did we?"

Tommy sniffed loudly. "He couldn't take it. He wasn't cut out for the army, soft little git like 'im. I should nevva 'ave pissed on 'is bed like that though...I..I.. dream about that sometimes... "

Carrie's ears pricked up at this. Walter was the name that Tommy would call out whenever he had bad dreams. She had always assumed he had been a soldier killed during the war, a comrade in Tommy's regiment, killed in action fighting for king and country. In her imagination, she had pictured Walter and Tommy heroically battling against the Germans in some far off war torn battlefield. She put her hand to her mouth as the shock hit her. She should have known better. Tommy had bullied that poor young man, just as he had bullied her all these years. Tommy had driven that poor boy to take his own life. A tear rolled down her cheek and she knew in that moment what she had to do.

Carrie picked up Tommy's insulin syringe and tried to remember how many units he had. Then she told herself grimly that it didn't matter. Tommy had two different kinds of insulin to take. He had a fast acting insulin that he needed during the day that worked swiftly to lower his blood sugar levels every time he ate, and a slow acting insulin that he had to take at night, that would keep his blood sugar levels steady throughout the night while he slept. Carrie tried to remember which one to use. She knew that the alcohol that Tommy had consumed would already have lowered his blood sugar levels, and if his blood sugar levels fell too far, he would slip into a coma and maybe die without treatment. Would Tommy wake up if she tested his blood glucose levels now? She didn't think so, but wasn't going to take the risk. If she used the slow acting insulin that Tommy was supposed to use in the evening, would it take too long to...? She couldn't say it, not even to herself.

She wanted it over quickly, and reasoned that in Tommy's drunken state it would be an easy mistake for him to make if he had been capable of giving himself his own insulin. She picked a site on his beer belly that she felt he could have reached himself. She was suddenly very calm. He did not stir when she gently pulled his trousers down to reach his stomach. She picked up the rapid insulin and she filled the syringe as far as it would go. She had not ever injected her husband before. When he was first diagnosed, the doctor had encouraged her to practise injecting an orange. He had said it was important that she knew what to do, just in case she had to do the injections one day. She hoped she could remember what she had been taught. Fill the syringe. Push a little tiny droplet of insulin out to release any air bubbles. Her hands trembled a little but she injected her husband's belly with a massive overdose. "Good bye, Tom" she said softly. She kissed her husband once on the forehead.

Tommy Miller would never raise his hand to his long-suffering wife again.

Sarah had been surprised when she came home to find the flat in total darkness. "Mum?" she called out, "Mum, are you in?" it wasn't yet 10'0'clock. She had been to visit Suzy. She had not stayed late, because she had to be up early for work next day. It was unusual for the flat to be so dark and quiet. A prickle of fear ran down her spine. She called out again, louder and more urgent this time.

"I'm in here"

Sarah raced to the living room, snapping on the light. Her mother was still sitting slumped on the floor. Carrie held her hands over her eyes as they slowly adjusted to the light. Then she looked up at her beautiful daughter.

Sarah saw her father, still and quiet on the couch. "Oh God, mum, what happened?"

Sarah listened incredulously as her mum wearily told her the full story. "He's dead. I killed him," Carrie said, unnecessarily. Sarah crouched down in front of her mother and gently held her by the shoulders. She looked her straight in the eyes. She spoke very slowly and quietly, as if speaking to a child. Her mother, she could see, was in deep shock. She had to protect her. She would not let her throw her life away over her father. He did not deserve such a sacrifice. She had already wasted too much time on him already. "Listen to me, mum. You did not kill that man. It's all going to be alright, I promise. Here's what we are going to do"

Carrie Miller stood by her daughter's side at her husband Tommy's funeral. It was a small gathering, only a handful of people had come along to pay their respects. Joycie and her husband Bob had come along to offer Carrie support. She had been very grateful for their kindness. Suzy was there of course, to keep Sarah's spirits up. Carrie tried her best to maintain an air of quiet dignity throughout the service. The crematorium was very beautiful and peaceful, and the vicar who held the service had spoken of Tommy as a family man who would be sadly missed by his loving wife and daughter Sarah. Carrie had felt mildly hysterical at that, and had felt Sarah squeeze her arm until she regained control.

Sarah had told her mother that morning that she needed to remain calm, if they could get through today, they could get through anything. Sarah gave her mums arm an encouraging squeeze, and Carrie swallowed hard and held her head up high.

Sarah had let the hot tears course down her face when they played the hymn abide with me. She watched her father's coffin glide slowly through the curtains in the tiny little crematorium.

Jonny held her hand. He misunderstood her tears. She was not crying for the father that she had lost. She was crying for a father she had never had in the first place.

Suzy stood with her mum and dad but came over to Sarah after the service. She did not say anything; she just put her arms around her beloved friend and held her tight.

After the service , as they all stood outside looking at the floral tributes,Tommy's friend, Frank Gloucester had come over to Carrie and Sarah and much to Carrie's surprise, had solemnly shook her hand. She could not speak. Her voice had got lost beneath the giant lump in her throat. He had seemed genuinely upset when Sarah had telephoned him to tell him of Tommy's death. He had felt very guilty for bringing the beer on his visit and for being one of the last people to see him alive. He had apologised profusely to Sarah over the phone, and had sent a huge reef on the day of the funeral. He had sat at the back of the crematorium during the service with his head bowed.

Sarah had been magnificent. She had dealt with everything, and Carrie had let her. By the time all the questions had been answered and the funeral arrangements had finally been made, Sarah had almost convinced Carrie that it had all been a terrible accident. Carrie did not want to admit to herself what she had done. At first, there had been a blissful numbness. It cushioned the enormity and hid her from the terrible truth. People had thought Carrie was so upset and shocked because she suspected Tommy had committed suicide. The police did not think there were any suspicious circumstances surrounding the death. They had to investigate of course. However, they were satisfied that no foul play had taken place. They spoke to Frank, who admitted he had taken Tommy beer as a present. They spoke to the district nurse who frequently visited, and she stated that Tommy was fiercely independent regarding his diabetes and insisted on doing his own insulin injections. As there was no suicide note, accidental death was a possibility, although suicide was of course a consideration. In the end however, suicide could not be proven and the cause of death had been registered as death by misadventure.

Carrie felt as if she was living in slow motion. She was almost sleep walking through the days and barely remembered the funeral. She had not cried since the day Tommy had died.

Sarah was very worried about her mother. She had not breathed a word about how her father really died to anyone. Only she and her mother knew the secret. It was safer that way, she had told her mother firmly. Don't go getting all - hysterical and guilty she had told Carrie. Sarah had made her mother promise never to tell a living soul.

 It was odd listening to people being sympathetic, and telling her that they were sorry for her loss. Sarah felt nothing but relief that the vicious old bastard was gone. She hoped with all her heart that her mum would snap out of her grief and guilt, and realise that she was finally free at last. Their secret had to remain just that, a secret. Her father had ruined her mother's past. It would be over her dead body if he ruined her future too. Sarah felt a twinge of guilt about keeping such a massive secret from Jonny. She shared everything with him, and he had told her all about his life. She knew that this was one thing she would never be able to divulge. More than anything, she feared his disapproval. She was not prepared to lose his love and respect. Her father had taken so much already, Sarah felt she could not risk sharing this dark secret. She had still not been able to share with Jonny just how violent her father had been. It was too painful to put into words. Maybe he would have understood but Sarah was not prepared to take the risk. If he despised her for what she had covered up, her life would crumble. It was something she would have to bear alone.

Carrie Miller finally cried three weeks after the funeral, when she received a letter from the Brewery. It said that Tommy had a life insurance policy that had been deducted from his wages every week. She had not known that Tommy had a life insurance policy. He had never told Carrie what he did with his wages, and she had always assumed that most of it had been drunk away in one pub or another. Along with the letter, there was a very generous cheque. She would never have to worry about money ever again. Her tears were not unhappy tears. They were tears not quite of joy, but of anticipation of her new life that was just about to unfold.

By the time that Sarah had come home from work however, Carrie was wracked with fresh guilt. She showed Sarah the letter, and the cheque, and told her tearfully that she didn't want the money, it was blood money, and she didn't deserve a penny of it. She wanted Sarah to take it all. "Use it to get married to your lovely Jonny" Carrie said between sobs, "I can't touch it, it would be wrong"

Carrie had never seen Sarah so cross or more determined. "Listen to me mum!" she had said, holding her mother firmly by the shoulders and giving her a little shake. "Every pound of that money represents a bruise dad gave you! You've earned that money a hundred fold! Of course you deserve it! You know, if you hadn't done what you had to do to dad, I would have killed him myself one of these days. No, don't look at me like that. He was a vile cruel excuse of a human being, who caused us nothing but pain. I was shocked that you managed to pluck up the courage to do it yourself, mum. Shocked, but amazed at your courage. I don't feel guilty that he's dead, and you are not to feel guilty, either. I love you; I will always protect you… I will not take it mum. It's yours. You put it in the bank first thing in the morning you daft cow, and let it give you the peace of mind you've never had before." Sarah smiled then and kissed her mother on the forehead. Carrie sobbed in her daughters arms. She knew she would do as her daughter asked.

Carrie had been to the bank as she promised Sarah. She deposited the cheque into her bank account. Once the cheque cleared, she transferred half of the money into Sarah's saving's account. She did not tell Sarah until the money was safely deposited. Sarah had cried, but hugged her mother gratefully. She knew exactly what she was going to do with her newfound wealth.

It had taken a while, but Nina had found out the horrible truth eventually. The drunken leering man had not made much sense at first, and had breathed beer fumes all over her and Lucy. Eventually one of his friends who were still fairly sober had joined them too. Slowly Nina had pieced together what had been going on. They had thought she was a porn star! She had laughed at first, thinking it was a hideous mistake, or some kind of sick joke. When one of the men had leered at her and said she looked very fuckable in her nurse's outfit, and described exactly what she had done whilst wearing it, she had gone cold. Her face had become redder and redder as realisation dawned on her. Oh my God, this had to be Billy's doing! The lying, treacherous bastard! She could not, did not want to believe it. At first, she did not fully understand, but then the penny finally began to drop. All the kinky outfits. Always insisting they do it in the bedroom. Him always wearing a mask, so he could not be recognised! How could she have been so naïve, so fucking stupid?

She had dragged Lucy back to her flat and searched the bedroom. Eventually, she had found the camera, hidden in the new bookshelf that he had made for her. Now she was sitting in the flat with Lucy, with a large vodka and tonic in her hand. She was absolutely mortified when she found the recording equipment and had become hysterical. It had taken Lucy a long time to calm her. Now she was icily calm, but still felt murderous. "What are you going to do?" her friend, looking pale and shocked, asked her eventually.

Nina looked up from her Vodka and tonic, smiled grimly and said coldly "I'm going to make him wish he had never been born"

It had taken a little time to set her plans in motion, and Nina had found it difficult to act normally, and pretend to Billy that everything was the same as usual. However, Nina was a firm believer in the old saying that revenge is a dish best served cold, and when she finally put her plan into action her patience had paid dividends and she was delighted with the way things turned out.

Billy had come home from work late on Friday night, smelling of engine oil, tired and hungry. His stomach rumbled as he turned his key in the lock and the delicious aroma of a chicken casserole wafted towards his nostrils. Nina was a good old stick really, he thought appreciatively. Not only did she have a fantastic pair of knockers, but she could cook as well. He told her he was going for a nice long soak in the bath before dinner.

He added, to keep her sweet, that the grub smelled lovely. He grinned when she said she had a special surprise for him later, and he felt something begin to stir under his greasy overalls. "I bet you have, you dirty bitch," he said, leering at her.

Nina had set everything in place. She had made a real effort. It was important that Billy was relaxed, and did not suspect anything. Last time Billy had had sex with her, he had told her he wanted to experiment with a bit of bondage. She had gritted her teeth, but meekly agreed. I'll give him bondage, the bastard, she thought to herself as she heard the bath running. She did one more check to make absolutely sure that things were ready, then she went to check that the food wasn't burning.

Billy had not been sure about being tied up at first. He liked to be the one in control. He was quite comfortable with tying Nina up, and the punters loved all the kinky stuff. The rougher he was, and the kinkier the outfits were that he made Nina wear, the more they liked it, and the more Mucky Micky would pay. Nina Had however, been very persuasive. She had told him over dinner that she would get so turned on, she would go wild, and she had promised she would only use silk scarves and would stop at any time if he did not enjoy it. "Please Billy" she had whispered in his ear, sitting on his lap at the dinner table and fondling him provocatively. I really will make it worth your while..." as she spoke, she moved her hands between his legs and he felt himself grow hard. Nina smiled, and led him into the bedroom, their half-eaten supper still on their plates.

Billy was lying naked, tied to the bed. She had told him that if he wanted to wear a mask, he could, but had told him to lie on the bed first, and let her spoil him. He had not put the camera on yet, so he decided to let her do what she wanted. He could always put the mask on later. She would have to go and tidy herself up at some point he told himself. Plenty of time to switch on the camera and put on the bloody mask so no one could recognise him in the blue movies. For now, he would just lie back and let her spoil him. Nina had produced a blindfold. Despite himself, Billy had become very aroused. He laid back, his arms above his head, his legs spread eagled. Nina had tied the scarves around his ankles, too, and had fastened the scarves securely to the bedposts. She put the blindfold on him, and told him to relax and enjoy himself. He quivered in anticipation, wondering what the saucy little minx was up to. She really was an old goer, was Nina. She had smothered his naked body in kisses, and he had loved it, groaning in pleasure, relaxing on the bed.

Billy felt Nina tighten the scarves around his ankles, and then she quickly moved up and put something hard and cold around his wrists. "What's that?" he said nervously. Too late. The handcuffs were fastened, and he could not escape. "What are you doing!" he shouted, wriggling and trying in vain to free himself. He didn't like this game now, not one bit, she had gone too far and he began to panic. "Let me go, right now! Nina, this ain't funny! You said silk scarves! What's wiv the fucking hand cuffs?"

While he struggled behind his blindfold, he had not noticed Nina move down his body. She was silent, and that scared the shit out of him. He was suddenly aware that Nina had his knob in her hands. Oh Christ, what was she doing? He had gone limp, and he was sweating. He felt beads of sweat trickling down his cheeks from under his blindfold. He really couldn't see a fucking thing. He felt her tie something around his meat and two veg. At last, she spoke.

"I wouldn't struggle, if I were you," Nina said, calmly. "I have just tied cheese wire round your bollocks" she added, matter of factly. "The cheese wire is rigged up to a pulley system. If you wriggle or struggle, the wire will tighten up, and you will be cut off in your prime... neutered. Which, really, is what you deserve, you horrible little shit! . I'm going to leave you now, for a while, anyway. Give you a bit of time to think about what a treacherous little weasel you are. I know about the camera, you slimy piece of scum! In fact, we are on camera right now. This should make a good film, shouldn't it? Think I'll invite all my mates round. We can have a good old laugh. How do you like that, eh Bill? Mind you, there's not much to see right now... I've seen bigger things crawl out of cabbages!"

Billy was furious and couldn't help himself, he struggled to get up. He gasped in pain, as he felt something cut into his nether regions. She really had done it, she wasn't bluffing!

"Get it off me, you bitch!" Billy screamed. Nina didn't reply. She had gone.

Billy lay very still, afraid of moving a muscle. The room was eerily quiet, and every muscle and tendon in his body ached now. He had cramp in his back from holding his position, and he was sure his cock was bleeding. He couldn't be sure how long he had lain there, but he estimated it to be at least an hour. He began to worry that Nina would never return, and had left him chained to this poxy bed to die. He felt his stomach growl too, as he had not finished his supper. He had visions of bleeding to death and he took deep breaths and tried hard not to panic.

Billy had finally nodded off, and awoke with a start. He let out a cry of pain, as he had moved unwittingly and the cheese wire had cut into him again. He heard a noise. "Nina! Is that you?

Look, I'm sorry! Really, I am! Let me go! Please babe, I promise, I'll make it up to you! I'm in agony! let me go!"

Billy squinted at the bright light as Nina pulled off the blindfold. For a few moments, he could not see a thing as his eyes adjusted to the bright light. As he began to focus again, he realised that he and Nina were not the only ones in the room.

Gathered around the bed stood Jonny Mason, Sarah Miller and Suzy Pond. Then, from behind them all, came another figure.

It was Victor Mason. He waved to Billy laying helpless and naked, tied down on top of the bedcovers. "Hello Billy" Victor Mason said at last. "Remember me?"

Billy was still naked and tied to the bed when the police arrived to arrest him. Jonny had looked murderous and Suzy had sworn at him and screamed at him, asking where her money was. Sarah had merely looked disgusted. Victor had stood quietly with his arms folded and smiled as the police officer untied him, made Billy put some clothes on and led him out to the waiting police car.

Nina sagged into an armchair when the police had left. Sarah had made everyone cups of tea. Nina smiled gratefully. She did not feel able to do it herself. Her legs had gone wobbly. She had searched the flat on the day she had found the hidden camera. She had found the holdall that Billy had used in the robbery hidden at the back of the wardrobe. Inside had been Victor's wallet, and a knife. Victor's business card had still been inside the wallet.

Jonny had been delighted when Nina had telephoned him, and explained who she was, and Nina had been only too happy to arrange rooms in the hotel where she worked when Jonny had agreed to help her set up a cunning plan.

CHAPTER SEVEN

Jonny and Sarah had found Victor the night he was stabbed. He was lying in a pool of his own blood when they came home from the pictures. The film they had chosen to go and see had been pretty awful, and they had decided to leave half way through after Jonny had whispered in Sarah's ear that he had seen a better film floating on top of an oily puddle. Thank God, they had gone straight home, he thought briefly, as he rushed to his father's side. Truffle was loyally lying beside him, with his head resting firmly on his blood stained shirt. Jonny had had to prize the dog off Victor in order to check that his father was still alive. Poor Truffle became frantic, and struggled to go back to Victor's side. Truffle's fur was caked in Victor's blood.

Sarah called the ambulance. Poor Truffle became frantic again when the ambulance crew arrived, and asked that any pets be removed from the room, and when Jonny shut him in the living room, he began to howl, and scratched frantically at the panelled door to get back to his beloved master. The ambulance man had added ruefully after attending to Victor that Truffle had done a fantastic job of guarding his master. The pressure he had inadvertently applied to Victors wounds had helped to stem the bleeding, and had almost certainly stopped Victor from bleeding to death.

Jonny sat, looking pale and anxious in the long corridor while surgeons worked on his father. Sarah sat by his side, holding his hand and trying to reassure him. They sipped the vile luke warm greyish tea from the vending machine. Neither of them wanted it, but it gave them both something to focus on. It was a long night.

Sarah used the telephone in the long hospital corridor and called her mum to tell her what had happened. Her mum had been a star, and said she would do anything she could to help. Jonny asked Sarah if she could think of anyone who would go to the house and look after Truffle. Sarah knew her mum would do it, but she also knew that her mum was a bit nervous of dogs. "What about Marlayna?" Sarah said.

Marlayna had rushed to the hospital as soon as she heard. Sarah had given her Victors door keys. She had picked them up off the hall table when the ambulance man suggested they would need them. Victor was still in surgery. The knife had pierced his intestines and the surgeon was concerned that it may have perforated his bowel. Septicaemia was a danger he had said grimly. The next forty- eight hours would be critical.

Marlayna said she would go to the house and take care of Truffle. She would stay with him, and clean up the house as soon as the police allowed it. She also promised to pack a bag for Victor and bring it back to the hospital as soon as she was needed.

The police wanted to speak to Victor as soon as he regained consciousness. They pestered the doctors and nurses but it was a full week before Victor was well enough in intensive care. Jonny insisted that he be present. "Take your time, Sir," the officer said to Victor gently. Victor was still very weak and looked deathly pale. "Did you get a good look at the person who did this to you?"

Victor turned towards Jonny and said quietly "Yes.. I..recognised him. I'm so sorry, Jon. The man who did this to me...It was Billy."

Jonny could not take it in. Billy? How could his so called friend do something like this? It was despicable. He had become very angry, and had to leave the room. He should have listened to Sarah. She had never trusted Billy. If he ever saw him again he would kill him with his bare hands.

Suzy Pond had had a straightforward pregnancy. The neighbours, of course, had all had a bloody good gossip at first. An unmarried mother was always a good excuse to set tongues wagging. Suzy had told anyone who gave her dirty looks to mind their own fucking business. They all wanted to know who the father was, the nosy old bats. Suzy smiled to herself. She could just imagine the field day they would have if they only knew. Billy the bastard had scarpered. She had been shocked to her marrow when Sarah had told her what he had done to Jonny's dad. She did not think even he would sink that low. Poor Jonny had been absolutely devastated. Bless him, he had even apologised to Suzy for introducing Billy to her in the first place, as if he was somehow responsible for all the terrible things that Billy had done.

Her mum Joycie had told all the neighbours scathingly that until she asked them for money for the baby's keep, they should shut their nosy traps, as it was nothing to do with any of them. Suzy's dad did not have to say anything. All the neighbours knew better than to say anything about his beloved Angel within earshot. No one was a match for Suzy's dad, Suzy thought proudly. She considered herself lucky, really. She had had a narrow escape where Billy was concerned and as for her parents, well they had been bloody brilliant. Her dad had put her name down for a council flat, but in the meantime, they had redecorated her bedroom and made it look fresh and welcoming for her. Her dad had bought her a lovely navy blue carrycot pram. Her mum had been frantically knitting and had spent every spare penny she had on baby clothes. Sarah had kept her well supplied with company when she needed it and bottles of vinegar, that Suzy craved on everything. They had joked together that the baby would come out pickled.

Eleanor Parish had been wonderful, really understanding, and had told Suzy that if she wanted her old job back after the baby was born, she would make sure that it was available. She even said she would try to arrange for Suzy to return to work part time, if she wanted. Suzy had been very grateful about that, and her mum had said she would be only too pleased to look after the little one if Suzy wanted to go back. It all seemed to be falling into place, and when Suzy went on maternity leave, she whiled away the days sitting with her feet up contentedly, splashing vinegar on her cheese on toast and reading the latest copy of Woman's Own.

Suzy's waters broke in the lift. She had only popped out to buy another magazine. The baby was six days overdue, and Suzy was restless. Her mum had offered to go to the shops for her, but Suzy had said the fresh air would do her good. As she looked at the mess on the lift floor, Suzy thought bashfully that the caretaker was going to love her, having to mop that lot up. She waddled her way back home again as quickly as she could, and her mum called an ambulance.

It had been a long labour. Suzy was so relieved when it was all over, that she almost forgot to ask if it was a boy or a girl. At last, a smiling midwife placed her baby daughter in her arms, and Suzy kissed her beautiful little head.

"Mum, look at Ellie May" Suzy said in a worried voice, the day after she had given birth. She was sitting up in bed in the small hospital ward. She hated hospitals, and could not wait to go home. She had had to have a lot of stitches, however, and felt weary and sore after the long labour. She wondered how women managed to have large families. She never ever wanted to go through that again. As if the stitches were not bad enough, her boobs felt like melons and she couldn't get to grips with breast feeding. Motherhood was definitely not a piece of cake. She looked over at her own mother now with new respect.

"I can't stop looking at her. She's gorgeous," said a besotted Joycie. She was such a proud nana, Suzy thought, tearfully.

"No mum, really look at her. Something's not right with her. I don't think she's normal"

Three days after the birth, Suzy was dying to go home, but the doctor's had told her that they needed to run a few more tests on the baby. Nothing to worry about, they had said, it was just routine. Suzy had not been convinced. She was worried. They had done endless bloody tests since the birth. The baby looked different from the other babies, her ears were tiny compared to the little boy in the next bed, and her mouth, her tiny little rosebud mouth, was well, tiny. Suzy held Ellie May in her arms protectively, and kissed her head. She was a bit floppy when she held her. Suzy had felt such a rush of love when she had held her in her arms for the first time, but now she couldn't help comparing her to the other babies on the ward. Ellie May was having trouble feeding, and the nurses kept whisking her out of sight. Suzy had caught one of the nursing sisters examining Ellie Mays hands.

Suzy had been told that a paediatrician would be coming to speak to her later today. Joycie tried her best to reassure her daughter, but Suzy was getting frantic. It was almost a relief when the doctor finally appeared. Looking concerned, he pulled the curtains around Suzy's bed, sat down beside her and held her hand.

Very gently, he explained to Suzy that Ellie May had Down Syndrome.

Suzy felt numb with shock. She could not speak. Her mum and dad sat at either side of the bed, staring blankly at the doctor. The doctor began saying that the baby would need monitoring, as many Down syndrome babies were born with heart conditions. He had said so far they had been fortunate, and no heart defects had been detected. Then he said the words that made Suzy's dad start shouting. The doctor suggested that Suzy might want to consider adoption as she was a young unmarried mother and the child would require constant, lifelong care. "She will probably never walk or talk coherently" the doctor stated bluntly, "and she might have all sorts of serious health problems"

"So, because she has a mental handicap, you think we should just cast her aside? Is that what you're saying?" Bob Pond spat out furiously. The doctor coloured, and looked embarrassed.

"No, of course I'm not suggesting that…but a child with this condition is a lifelong commitment…"

"Any bloody child is a lifelong commitment!" Bob Pond interrupted furiously.

"I'm merely suggesting that there are options, that's all. I will leave you with some leaflets. I realise it is a huge shock and you will need time to come to terms with it. I will come back and speak to you later." With that, he stood up and hastily left the room.

William Donald Jameson pleaded not guilty. Billy had never heard his full name read out before, and he stood in the dock looking bewildered. His brief had advised that if he pleaded guilty and showed remorse for what he had done, he would receive a reduced sentence from the judge.

Billy decided not to play the game. His bravado had deserted him as he stood before all the people he had hurt though, and he was scared. Really scared. He had felt as if he was a gangster in a movie up until now. He knew deep down that he would not get away with all he had done, but even as a little kid, he had always protested "It wasn't me" More often than not, he would turn on the charm and everything would be okay. He had hoped that he could do the same in front of the jury. It had all seemed a bit unreal. His life had somehow spiralled out of control, and he could not stop it. He had never been inside prison before. Being on remand until his trial had been terrible. The thought of having to go back there made his stomach constrict in fear.

He could not get the disappointed look of his mother Violet's face out of his mind. He had taken it for granted that she would support him, and always stick up for him. After all, he was her son. When she had shook her head sadly and sobbed, he had tried to put his arms around her. He had been shocked to the core when she had slapped his face as hard as she could, and

171

said that he was dead to her now. "How could you, Billy? How could you do that to your own friend's father? Jonny has always been such a good friend to you! Then, as if that wasn't bad enough, disappearing without a word all that time! Did you ever think how me and your dad felt? And that poor girl Nina! I am so ashamed. I'm disgusted! As far as I'm concerned, I don't have a son anymore! And don't expect me to visit you when you get locked up, cos I won't come. Not now Bill, not ever! I wash my hands of you! You're a stupid, stupid boy, and you've broken your muvver's heart!"

Billy was shocked. His mother had never looked so cold. She was broken, he could see that, and he needed to fix her, to make her believe he was still her little boy. She had always doted on her sons. It had always been easy for Billy in particular to wrap her around his little finger. His father had always been jealous of the closeness between them, and Billy had not been upset that he had not bothered to show up or offer any help. He had not even been surprised when Billy had been arrested. He had always thought the worst of Billy. His mum though, he had always counted on his mum. He needed her to be on his side, to make everything all right the way she always had. He felt panic rise in the pit of his stomach. He had never felt so alone. "You don't mean it mum...Please! Say you don't mean it! I know I've been an idiot, I'm sorry..." but Billy's mother had already turned away and was no longer listening. Billy cried then. Reality had kicked in. He wept bitter salty tears for the mother that he had lost.

He had been charged with aggravated burglary, attempted murder and making pornographic films with intent to sell and supply for money, contravening the obscene publications act of 1964. He had avoided the eyes of the gallery when the charges had been read out.

Nina did not know that Billy had invited several other women to her flat while she had been at work. She had to sit and listen as the full sordid story came out in court. She sat and tried to cling on to her dignity as all his grubby little secrets were flung around the courtroom, like tainted confetti. She wished with all her heart that she could wipe away the hideous pictures that were swimming around in her head as easily as wiping steam from her bathroom mirror. She knew that the filthy images would remain imbedded in her memory forever. She listened with tears in her eyes, but held her head high. She would not let that bastard beat her. She clung to the last shreds of dignity as if it were a life jacket.

Billy could feel Nina's eyes boring into him, full of loathing as the court heard how Billy had got the other girls tipsy, had sex with them and made his grubby little films. Even raunchier than the films he had made with Nina. Billy had enjoyed a threesome with the two girls. They too were up in the gallery of the court, and were now glaring down at him.

Nina felt so dirty and ashamed. All the sordid details of her sex life were being discussed for the world to hear. She wanted to run away and hide, curl up and die of embarrassment. She was deeply touched when Suzy, Billy's ex-girlfriend had come over to her on the first day of the trial and hugged her. She had not seen her since Billy's eventful arrest, but they had spoken a few times on the telephone, especially once they had found out the date of Billy the Bastard's trial. Suzy had stayed close to Nina all through the trial, and they had both been relieved to find they got on really well.

Suzy had liked this plucky woman as soon as she had met her. She thought her revenge with the cheese wire had been a work of sheer genius, and had nothing but respect for her. It was a small comfort to Nina that a cheer went up in the gallery when Nina had to describe the bondage with cheese wire incident. The judge had not been amused however, and had demanded order in his court. Nina felt comforted knowing she had made a new friend in Suzy, and that she at least had some support from the gallery.

Nina and Suzy had stood side by side, united together outside the courthouse during the lunch break. Suzy was shocked and very surprised when a pinched faced woman approached them. It was Billy's mother. "I .. I hope you don't mind me coming over. I just wanted to say….I am so sorry"

It was Suzy that reached out first and put her arms around the poor woman. Nina had patted Billy's mother reassuringly on the back. The three of them hugged then, and cried together.

Suzy's mum and dad were not happy when they saw Suzy talking to Billy's mother. Joycie in particular could not forgive her for giving birth to the person responsible for so much heartache, and told Suzy exactly how she felt. "Give her a break, mum" Suzy said quietly. "I must admit, I didn't like that poor cow much when I first saw her, but it took a lot of guts for her to come over to us and apologise. It's not her fault that Billy is such a scumbag. She's been cheated out of such a lot. Her other son has moved to find work and she hardly ever hears from him, her old man is neither use nor ornament and she feels so alone. I wonder.. mum, should I tell her about Ellie May?"

Suzy sat with Violet Jameson in a little coffee shop near the Court. Suzy's mum and dad had not been happy about it, but Suzy felt that Violet should know she had a grand- daughter. Suzy had not named Billy as Ellie May's father on the birth certificate, but she hoped that Violet would believe her when she said that Billy was the father, and that she would be pleased. Over their second cup of tea, Suzy tentatively opened her handbag and brought out a photograph. "Vi, I want you to look at this photo. It's... it's my daughter, Ellie May." Suzy watched carefully as Violet studied the grinning little face in the photograph. Violet smiled widely. She did not seem fazed that Ellie May was a Down syndrome child. "She's gorgeous." She said, still looking at the picture. Suzy took a deep breath, and then said quickly before she could change her mind, "I was hoping you'd say that. She's your grandchild."

Billy stood up in his best charcoal grey suit while the charges were read aloud and he did his best to look penitent. He could not quite manage it. He was still confident that he would be found not guilty and walk free from the courtroom. He had pictured himself punching the air in jubilation, cheering at the silly little slags in the gallery and waving defiantly towards Jonny and his father Victor.

As the foreman of the jury stood and pronounced a guilty verdict to all counts as charged, Billy felt his bowels begin to squirm. He could hear a roaring in his ears, and he wondered briefly if he was about to pass out. He clung to the edge of the stand to steady himself.

The judge sentenced Billy to ten years. Ten bloody years! Billy sagged at the knees and had to be helped down to the cells. He was numb with shock and did not really take in much else. He was put in a prison van and driven away. He closed his eyes, but could still see the jubilant looks of Jonny and his father, and hear the cheers that Nina, Sarah and Suzy let out at the top of their voice. He could still feel his mother's disappointed tearful eyes boring into his face as he was taken down.

Billy sat in his cell. At the moment, he was alone, but there was to be another prisoner joining him soon. He was trying to adjust to the daily prison routine and the smell of cabbage and bad cooking, sweat, bodily functions and confinement. The stale air in the cramped cell was making him feel nauseous. He had decided to keep his head down and keep out of trouble. He was still reeling with shock after the reality of his sentence had been explained to him. His brief had spent a long time with Billy, explaining the jist of what the judge had said. At the time in the court room, Billy had been too numb with shock, and had not taken any of it in after he had heard that he was going to be locked up for ten years.

His lawyer, Mr Tompkins had explained that he was now a Category B prisoner. He had been given a Discretionary Life sentence tariff. Although he had not actually murdered Victor, the judge had said that he had wounded with intent to kill, as he had stabbed Victor seven times. The stab wounds he had inflicted had caused irrevocable damage and Victor would never fully recover from his multiple injuries. He had also added that Billy's gambling addiction was an aggravating factor and stated that in his opinion he would remain a real threat to the public as he would need to fund his gambling addiction. There were no mitigating circumstances to be considered in Billy's favour. The judge had not taken kindly to Mr Tompkins explaining about the loan shark, commenting that surely the threat of reprisals would eventually push Billy into committing further crimes.

Billy's brief had explained all this to him, and had added that he would not be eligible for parole for many years to come, and even if he did become eligible for parole, he would have to serve his tariff. That was his minimum sentence. Billy had panicked at this news, and it had taken quite a while to calm him down. He had not realised that he would not be automatically released at the end of his Discretionary life sentence. The parole board would have to decide whether he was still considered a danger to the public. He could be behind bars until he rotted.

Billy sat breathing deeply with his head in his hands. He wanted his mum. Her voice was still ringing in his ears. She had come to see him, had travelled for hours to get to this God forsaken place they had brought him to. He had been delighted at first, thinking that she had forgiven him, and that everything would be all right after all. Visitors were the only thing that kept the prisoners going. It was wonderful to have something to look forward to during the long tedious days of confinement.

At first, they had chatted, and Billy had felt better than he had felt for a very long time. Then she had taken out that revolting dog eared photograph of a mongol kid and come out with some cock and ball story about the kid being his! That stupid, conniving bitch Suzy had been whispering in her ear, and tried to pin this on him. Well no way! He could never father a kid like that!

Before he could stop himself, he had told his mum that the kid was nothing to do with him, and that she was a mug to be taken in by a sob story from slutty Suzy. He could not get the disgusted look his mother gave him out of his head. She had slapped his face and cried. She told Billy she was ashamed of him, and said she was a fool for expecting anything else from him. Then, she had stood up and turned away, and through her sobs had told him firmly that she would not be coming back, not ever. She sobbed that she had tried she had really tried. He really was dead to her now, she had said.

He took deep breaths, trying to let it all sink in. He couldn't believe his own mother would disown him like that, over a kid that wasn't even his. He called after her receding back, begging her to stay, but it was too late. He felt panic rising in his throat like bile. He had never felt so alone or desolate in his life. He was suddenly a child again, it was the first day of school and he was suffering separation anxiety like a four year old. "Muuuuum!" he screamed, "Mum! Come back! I didn't mean it!" The screws were over in an instant and he was led back to his cell, babbling and sobbing like a baby.

A shadow fell across his open cell door and he looked up. The screws had stayed with him for a long while, talking to him and trying to calm him down. They had said he needed time to adjust, to accept his sentence and stop being in denial. They had finally left him, alone and red eyed to think things over. A huge mountain of a man stood blocking the doorway. He was smiling at Billy. It was a cold, shark's smile. The man mountain's eyes were dead and almost reptilian. Billy swallowed hard, and heard his own heart thumping in his chest.

"My oh my, but you're a pretty one, aren't you?" the man mountain said quietly. Billy said nothing. His mouth was suddenly too dry to speak.

"Billy, isn't it?" the man mountain had a surprisingly well educated accent. "Welcome to the Nick, pretty boy. It's a shame you won't stay pretty in here for too long. My name is Maurice Chambers. My friends in here call me Little Mo. Some in here call me Pyscho...only once, mind you. They never try to take liberties twice.... You, on the other hand, can call me Sir."

"Please!" Billy interrupted, finding his voice at last, "Please, I..I don't want no trouble. Please leave me alone" His voice was high pitched and whining. He could feel his already stinging eyes begin to well up again. He cleared his throat, and hoped he did not sound as shit scared as he felt.

He could feel the man mountains cold dead eyes boring into him, like laser beams. Then Little Mo studied his own fingernails, and grinned slowly at Billy. "Leave you alone? Now, where is the fun in that?" he said softly. "Oh...and by the way, pretty little Billy boy, Mr Nick Crowley said to say hello"

Marlayna had been quite magnificent Jonny had to admit. He had been slightly peeved at first when Sarah told him she had rung her, thinking that his dad would not want to worry anyone about the stabbing, but as ever Sarah was shrewd, and it had been an excellent decision. Marlayna had rallied round like a real trouper whilst Victor had been in hospital and had run about all over the place. She did everything willingly, was always cheerful, and said she was glad she could be useful. She had temporarily adopted Truffle, giving him a huge chewy bone as a reward for being a hero and helping to save Victor. Truffle had become something of a celebrity in the area, as the press had got hold of the story, and featured a very flattering photograph of the handsome freshly bathed Labrador in the local gazette, with the headline "Hero Hound Saves Master From Multiple Stabbing" Victor had been delighted to see the article, and Jonny had it framed. Truffle remained modest about his starring role, enjoyed all the extra treats and fuss he received and waited patiently for Victors return from hospital.

Marlayna fussed over Truffle and took him for long walks. She cooked for Jonny and brought hot nourishing food to the hospital for him and for Victor too once he could manage it. Hospital food had been just as bad as Victor had imagined it to be and he had visibly lost weight until Marlayna intervened. Jonny was spending every spare minute he could at Victor's bedside, and had had no time for cooking. Sarah had volunteered, but had to admit that her culinary skills would probably cause Victor to have a relapse. Carrie had shyly visited, and had brought fruit and newspapers. Victor had been very touched by everyone's concern. He said he was sorry to have caused so much bother, and ruefully told Jonny that he was never going to do his heroic act ever again. He had spent three weeks in intensive care. His lungs had collapsed, one knife wound had narrowly missed his heart and he knew that he had made a miraculous recovery. He fully intended to take things very easy from now on.

Marlayna had offered to mind the shop. She had not only worked all day there, with Truffle at her side but also kept Victor and Jonny's house tidy, washed clothes, and ferried clean pyjamas and fresh toiletries to the ward every evening. Victor was very grateful and surprised himself by looking forward to her daily visits far more than he cared to admit. When visiting time arrived, he had found himself looking anxiously at the door, hoping to see her smiling face appear, and light up the ward with her presence.

Victor sat up in his hospital bed, with Jonny at his bedside. Victor was wearing new pyjamas that Marlayna had bought. He was looking forward to her visit later. He was looking much more like his old self, much to Jonny's relief. Now he was growing stronger, Jonny felt it was time to broach a delicate subject. "Marlayna's been fantastic, hasn't she Dad?" he said, watching intently to gouge his father's reaction.

"Yes, she certainly has" Victor replied, looking suddenly delighted at the mention of Marlayna's name. "She's been a great help. You certainly know who your friends are, when the chips are down" he added, a bit sheepishly. Jonny leant forward in his hard hospital chair. "Dad" he said, speaking slowly and carefully, "Marlayna is not doing any of this out of mere friendship." He waited patiently for his dad to respond, and Victor looked at him in astonishment. "What do you mean?" Victor said, in a voice that he hoped was non-committal. Jonny sighed, in exasperation, and shook his head. "Dad, I am seriously beginning to think that Billy the Bastard did far more damage than multiple stab wounds. I think he must have addled your brains as well. Stop being thick, oh father of mine. It's so bloody obvious that Marlayna loves the very bones of you, you daft sod! She is a beautiful and lovely woman. I'm afraid that if you don't do the decent thing and ask her out on a proper date when you get out of here, I will have to put myself up for adoption"

"You mean, you wouldn't mind?" Victor said quietly.

"Mind? Why should I mind, you daft old git?"

"Well...I don't wan't you to think I'm being disloyal to your mother."

Jonny smiled. He loved his father so much. "Dad, I am a grown up now. Of course I don't bloody mind. I know how much you loved my mum, but I think it's time you moved on now." He gave his dad a little smile, and added, "I think it's about time you had a bit of happiness though, don't you?"

Victor couldn't speak. He just patted his son's hand, and managed to nod in agreement.

CHAPTER EIGHT

Suzy had been offered a ground floor three bedroom flat in Harold Laski House. Ellie May was nearly three and Suzy had lived with her mum and dad since the baby had been born. She had begun to think she would never have a place of her own. She was incredibly grateful to her parents, and had enjoyed having her mum around to help out with the baby but she thought it was high time she learned how to be independent. She had learned slowly to accept Ellie May, and had been very lucky that Ellie had been healthy. She had been terrified when she had read the leaflets that the doctors had given her in the hospital. The list of life threatening conditions that Down syndrome children were prone to had seemed endless.

Suzy had not wanted to go to sleep at first, fearing that her little baby would not be breathing when she awoke. It had taken a very long time for her to feel at ease with the baby. Suzy had accepted the offer of the flat at once, even though the thought of living alone was a bit daunting. The flat was in Percival Street, which was within spitting distance from King Square, where her mum and dad lived, and was right next to Brunswick Court where Sarah lived. She had been amazed to be offered three bedrooms. She was only entitled to two. The bedrooms were quite small, but she was still incredibly grateful. She could use the spare bedroom as a playroom when Ellie May got older, and for a guest room for the time being. Her brother, Robert had helped her dad to decorate the flat and get it ready for Suzy and Ellie May to move in.

As Suzy unlocked the front door, the smell of fresh paint filled her nostrils. Her dad stood behind her as she surveyed her new home. She had not seen it since the painting had begun. Her dad and brother had wanted it to be a surprise. Suzy was touched, but also afraid that her dad and brother would make a right pig's ear of things. Most men, Suzy told herself, were not exactly known for their interior design skills. "Well, what do you think?" Suzy's dad said anxiously.

Suzy was so choked up, she could not speak. The flat looked beautiful. It was bright, clean and perfect. The hall had been painted in pale beige that looked welcoming and cheerful. When Suzy had first viewed the flat, the hallway had been covered in red brocade wallpaper that was dark and oppressive. Suzy wandered into the living room, which had once had hideous orange flowers covering it from floor to ceiling. Now it had a modern pale duck egg blue paper, which was Suzy's favourite colour. The kitchen had a cheerful red and white theme, and Suzy's bedroom had a soothing pale green and white colour scheme. The bathroom was white, with new blue towels. It looked fresh and clean. Suzy could not stop beaming. Her dad held the door of the second bedroom, Ellie May's nursery, and said proudly "This is the biggest surprise for you, sweet heart. Me and Robert worked really hard on it. I hope you like it." He opened the door with a flourish, and said "Ta Dah!"

The room had been painted in bright primary colours. There was a new cot bed with a cheerful red yellow and blue patchwork quilt and matching pillow. Ellie May needed sides on her bed, so she would not toddle out and hurt herself in the middle of the night, and this was perfect. Around the walls, a painted rainbow arched across a field, and bright butterflies and blue birds flew amongst red, yellow, orange and pink flowers.

Suzy stood trying to take it all in, with tears streaming down her face. "I did a lot of research" Suzy's dad said enthusiastically, "Downs children like bright colours, and they need good visual stimulation, so I tried to make Ellie May's room as bright as I could. Robert did the mural. You know what he's like, all arty farty. Do you like the lamps?" he pointed to a red and white bedside lamp that was in the shape of a giant toadstool. Suzy was so choked up, she could not speak, but she nodded at her excited dad enthusiastically. There were fairy lights hanging on the wall, and another lamp in the corner of the room that looked like a bunch of multi coloured balloons. A comfy red armchair was next to it, and a chest of drawers and little wardrobe had been painted in rainbow colours too. In one corner was a small table and chair for Ellie May to sit at. Suzy rushed into her father's arms and hugged him half to death. "Oh dad, it's bloody perfect"

Suzy settled in to her new home remarkably quickly, although the first few days were a bit tricky. Joycie had cried for hours when Suzy left home with the baby. Joycie still thought of Ellie may as a baby. She still thought of Suzy as a baby, come to that. She had thoroughly enjoyed having the two girls living with her. She was going to miss them like mad. Even though she was only just around the corner, she fretted that Suzy would not be able to cope on her own with the baby. She told Suzy tearfully that she was only a phone call away, and added that she would come and stay over anytime.. "Mum, do give over. I'm five minutes away, it's not Australia, you silly mare!" she hugged her mother fondly, and fought back her own tears.

Despite herself, it was a big step, and she had never lived alone before. Now she was a mother. Not any old mother, either, but a mother with a daughter who had special needs. Ellie May was an absolute darling, but she was a handful. You could not take your eyes off her for a second. She required constant twenty-four hour care. It was all a bit scary, but she did not want her mum or dad to worry about her.

She had settled into a nice little routine, living with her parents. She had taken everything in her stride, and coped really well. She had fought almost daily battles with stupid ignorant people who sniggered and made comments when they saw Ellie May. She had almost had a stand up fight just a week ago when a young bloke in the park had told his daughter to come away from the Mongol kid, as if Down syndrome was some kind of contagious disease. She had learned how to appear confident, but it had been easy knowing that her mum and dad were always to hand. Now she had to learn how to cope alone. She knew her parents and Sarah would always help her out whenever she needed them, and that helped enormously.

Suzy had been pleasantly surprised that Billy's mother, Violet, had accepted Ellie May, and had become a constant visitor. It had been a bit awkward at first as her mum and dad had not approved, but even they had come round once they saw how much Violet loved being with little Ellie May.

Ellie May called Violet "Vi Lit" and loved to sit on her knee and sing nursery rhymes with her. Suzy really appreciated all the support she received from family and friends, but she needed to prove to herself that she could handle being a mum who was able to stand on her own two feet.

Her first night alone with Ellie May had been difficult. Ellie had been unsettled in the unfamiliar surroundings, and had cried for hours. It had not helped when a disgruntled next-door neighbour had given her dirty looks the next morning when she had gone out to her doorstep to bring her milk in. She had the same milkman, as her mum, and it had seemed very grown up to be bringing in her very first pinta on her first full day in her new home.

Greg, the milkman had given her a cheery wave and called out "Morning love!" As he came down the stairs, his empty crate rattling against the stair banisters. He saw the neighbour scowling at Suzy before he scuttled back inside his front door and slammed it shut. The noise of the slamming door made Suzy jump, and she nearly dropped her precious pint. She was dying for a cuppa. "I see you've met our prince charming then" Greg said with a grin, inclining his head towards the neighbour's door. Suzy nodded. "Don't think I'm flavour of the month at the moment. Ellie May kept everyone awake last night, I'm afraid."

"Don't let it worry you, love. No one's ever flavour of the month with old misery guts. He's only happy when he's moaning. Don't let him get to you. See you tomorrow, love" with that, he started to whistle cheerily and went back out to his milk float.

Despite her rocky start, Suzy soon got used to her new flat. Ellie May settled down after the first few nights and Suzy loved having a place of her own. She soon got into a routine, and got talking to some of the other young mum's who lived in the little block. None of the other tenants got on with Suzy's next-door neighbour, Mr Norris, or Narky Norris as Suzy called him. At one time or another, he had argued with just about everyone and the anti-Norris brigade was a common bond amongst all the other tenants.

Sarah came to visit whenever she could, and would stay over once a month or so. Sarah loved Ellie May, and the three of them had a great time together. Suzy had worried that she would feel lonely, but she hardly ever did. She saw her mum nearly every day, and her dad always popped in at weekends if she needed any little jobs doing. Her neighbours apart from Narky, were friendly and she even managed the odd night out with Sarah when her mum and dad baby sat for her. All in all, Suzy was content. She watched her sleeping little daughter, and her heart melted. This was definitely not how she had thought her life would turn out, she told herself as she lovingly stroked her daughters hair, but she realised she wouldn't change a bloody thing.

Suzy had been surprised and pleased when she received a long letter from Nina. They had stayed in touch since the trial, which seemed like another lifetime ago now, but Suzy realised guiltily that she had forgotten to tell Nina about moving into a place of her own. She owed Nina a letter. The letter from Nina had been delivered to her mum and dad's address, and Joycie had brought it round on one of her frequent visits.

 Nina wrote that she would be coming to London in two weeks' time, as she had an interview for a receptionist at a top London hotel. She wondered if Suzy would like to meet up. Suzy wrote back that evening when Ellie May was fast asleep, and said that yes; she would love to meet up. She added that if Nina needed a place to stay while she was in London, she was more than welcome to stay with her, as she had her own flat now, with a spare room. There was not a spare bed, she suddenly realised, but she did have a very comfy sofa. She put that bit as a P.S at the bottom of her letter. She put her new address carefully at the top of the letter, with her new telephone number, and posted it the next morning.

Nina had been delighted to accept. She rang Suzy as soon as she had read her letter and they had had a nice long chat. Her interview had been on a Thursday, and Suzy had persuaded her to stay all weekend. Nina was a bit pissed when she rung Suzy and pretty soon was pouring her heart out.

She told Suzy that her boss would probably be glad to get rid of her for a few days anyway. She had kept all her problems bottled up for such a long time; it had been blissful to finally unload them. Suzy didn't mind. She put her feet up and settled down to listen. Nina told her tearfully that life had been difficult for her after the trial, as everyone was gossiping about her again, and work at the hotel had become a nightmare. That was the trouble living on a small Island, she said sadly. She told Suzy it had felt like every pervert in the world had popped in to gawp at "Naughty Nina" and they all thought it was hysterically funny to call out lewd comments.

She had even become a bit of a tourist attraction, and people had pointed at her in the street. The manager of the hotel had not been amused, and the stress had made her ill. She had tried to ride it out, thinking that the locals would soon find something else to gossip about, but the damage had been done. Things were never the same she said, and she had lost the respect of the other members of staff. Her manager had thought he would try his luck and had cornered her in the chambermaids supply cupboard. He had not been happy when Nina had told him in no uncertain terms that she would not touch him even if he came gift wrapped with a purple bow tied round his knob.

Suzy had nearly choked with laughter at that point. She couldn't stand it anymore Nina said after her third glass of lambrusco. He was still making her life a misery, and so she had decided she needed a clean break. She had been looking for another job for over a year, but this one was the first interview she had been asked to attend in London. Suzy could hear Nina slurping her wine as she listened on the phone, and told her to make sure she packed a bottle or two in her suitcase, as they still had a lot of catching up to do.

Nina was delighted when she got the job in London, and so was Suzy. Suzy had asked Nina if she would like to stay with her in her flat until she got herself settled. She could do with the company and the rent she added laughing. Nina had accepted at once. London was an expensive place, and she couldn't afford so much as a cardboard box anywhere else. She had naively thought that on her new improved salary she would be able to find a nice little flat somewhere, maybe close to the hotel. Suzy had laughed out loud when Nina had said that. When Nina looked at a few properties, she realised why. Even a garden shed would have been out of her price bracket, rental costs were astronomical.

She had hoped that the hotel might have offered her a live in option, but it hadn't. Suzy had provided an answer to all her prayers. Suzy's little flat was so central Nina could hop on a bus or walk to the underground and be behind the reception desk in no time. The girls thought it would be only a temporary arrangement, as Suzy was worried about Nosy Narky Norris telling the Council that she had a lodger. The council did not like their tenants to sublet, especially if they were on any kind of benefits, but Suzy was finding it a real struggle to survive financially and this idea had struck her as an ideal solution.

Suzy had wanted to return to work when Ellie May was about six months old, and had fully intended doing so. Her mum had volunteered her services as baby sitter in chief when Suzy had been pregnant, and Miss Parish had offered Suzy her job back. However, when Ellie May was born with special needs, all Suzy's plans had changed. Looking after Ellie May was a full time job. She was a live wire right from the start. She did not sleep well, and now she was into everything. Suzy didn't think it was fair to palm her off on her mum. All babies were demanding, of course, but Ellie May was nearly three now, and heavy to carry around. She was the size of any other three year old, but was still in nappies and had only just started toddling. Suzy knew her mum and dad loved their granddaughter to bits, but there was no denying that she was even more of a handful than other young children were, and needed constant care. Suzy was always worn out by the time bedtime came around. She did not want to take advantage of her mum's good nature. Ellie May was physically and mentally demanding and Suzy's mum and dad were not as young as they were. Suzy would have loved to be financially independent and return to work, but was content to stay at home with her little girl. Having a lodger seemed like a perfect way to help her and Nina out.

Just as Suzy suspected, Miserable old Narky Norris started gossiping and interfering almost as soon as Nina had unpacked. Within three weeks, Suzy received a stern letter from Islington Council warning her of a breach in her tenancy agreement. They informed her that they would be sending a council officer round to investigate. Suzy's dad was incandescent with rage, and Suzy had to quite literally hold him back, as he wanted to go and ram his fist down Narky's nasty interfering throat. Actually, Suzy wanted to help him do it, but she had Ellie May to consider now, and calmly told her dad that she would speak to her health visitor.

"Dad, calm down" Suzy said, "I will speak to Hazel."

Hazel was Ellie May's health visitor. " You know she's as good as gold. Look how she helped set up the speech therapy for Ellie. I'd have had to wait ages for that appointment if she hadn't stepped in. If I have to, I'll play the I've got a Down syndrome child and I need help card!" Suzy's dad grinned. He had nothing but admiration for his fabulous resourceful daughter.

Much to Narky Norris's chagrin, Suzy smoothed things over with the council, and Nina was allowed to stay. Suzy looked suitably penitent when she got a lecture saying she should have informed the council before Nina moved in, but everything was fine. Suzy and Nina could relax at last. The arrangement worked like a dream for both of them, and Nina was delighted when Suzy said she could stay as long as she liked. Nina loved her new job, one of the hunky young waiters had already asked her out, and life was finally looking up.

Marlayna lay on the sun lounger and turned the page of her paperback novel. It was the first holiday she had been on for seven years, and here she was, lounging lazily in the Italian sun with Victor Mason. She had never been so happy in her entire life. She could not believe her good fortune. She had been reading a lovely holiday romance that she had bought at the airport, but she looked up and smiled now as Victor, already bronzed, handed her a large glass of sparkling white wine. He wore shorts but covered the scars on his chest with a crisp white tee shirt. "Ah, this is the life!" he said happily, as he plonked himself down on the lounger next to her.

They were relaxing on the balcony of their hotel room before getting ready for dinner. Marlayna thought that Victor was at last looking relaxed and almost back to his old self. The mere sight of him made her pulse quicken and her heart brimmed over with love for this darling man. The resort was by the edge of Lake Garda, and after dinner they were going to take a nice romantic stroll into the little town centre.

The evenings there had been magical. Fairy lights lit the pathway around the lakeside, and all the restaurants had little tables and chairs for diners to eat al Fresco by the water's edge. They were experimenting, and had tried as many different restaurants as they could. All of them so far had been wonderful. There were even several musicians strumming violins and singing romantic ballads to the diners as they ate. Marlayna had remarked to Victor on their first stroll that she did not care if the Italian baritone who was trying his best to serenade an elderly couple was reciting a shopping list, it still sounded romantic sung in Italian. Victor had posted many postcards home to Jonny and Sarah, and had even sent a couple of cards to Truffle. He told them all what a fabulous time they were having. He couldn't ever remember being so relaxed and happy. Well, not since Lydia had died, anyway. He was so glad he had taken the plunge and invited Marlayna out. They had settled into a very comfortable relationship, and he considered himself a very lucky man. This holiday had been incredible. He hadn't realised how badly he had needed a break, or how very much he had fallen in love with his gorgeous Marlayna.

So far, they had been on a day trip to Verona, and seen the famous Juliet balcony that Shakespeare wrote about in Romeo and Juliet. Victor had smiled and laughed his head off as Marlayna attempted the "Romeo, Romeo, where for art though Romeo?" speech in her delicious Polish accent. They both posed for photographs beside the bronze statue of Juliet." You have to touch the statue it is supposed to bring good luck!" Marlayna said, squinting at the information in her guidebook. They both roared with laughter, as poor Juliet had one highly polished bosom. "I can see she's been deeply touched by a hell of a lot of people" Victor said dryly.

They were looking forward to another day trip to Venice and Victor promised Marlayna a ride in a Gondola. He had laughed at her horrified expression when she had said "They cost the earth, it's a rip off, my friend Rula came and said the Gondoliers can spot a tourist a mile off!"

"I don't care" Victor said calmly, "You can't come all the way to Venice and not go on a Gondola. Don't worry about the money. Just enjoy it. If you're lucky, I'll even serenade you as we float along"

Victor Mason had received a letter on his first day back after his fabulous holiday. It had been put through the letterbox at the shop. Victor was puzzled, as he did not recognise the spidery handwriting on the envelope. It was simply addressed to "Mr V. Mason" It was from Billy's mother. She wrote;

Dear Mr Mason,

I hope you won't mind me writing to you, but I thought you had a right to know. I have told Suzy but I didn't think it was fair to her to have to tell you, so I am letting you know myself. The prison contacted me a few days ago to tell me that Billy was found dead in his cell. He hung himself and took his own life. I have not seen Billy since he first got sent down, and as far as I am concerned my son died the moment he did what he did to you. He would not accept Ellie May as his daughter and I could never forgive him for that, or all the terrible things he did to you and those poor girls. I am so sorry, and am ashamed to have been his mother. I could never forgive him, and Billy knew how I felt. Anyway, I say again I hope you won't mind me writing. I thought you and Jonny would want to know. I hope you are well now, and have a long and happy life.

Kind Regards,

Mrs Violet Jameson.

Wordlessly, Victor passed the notepaper to Jonny. Moments later, Jonny put the notepaper down, bowed his head and cried.

Sarah rang Suzy's doorbell and heard Ellie May trying to open the door. "Wait for me, Ellie!" she heard Suzy say behind the front door. Sarah couldn't help smiling. Bless her, she thought. Ellie May was always so pleased to see her. Sarah had been surprised that Suzy had not told her about Billy's suicide, but she understood when she had said defiantly that poor Violet had been distraught and the pair of them just wanted to get on with their lives. Nina had cried at the news, which had surprised Sarah even more. When Sarah told Suzy about the letter Victor had received from Violet, Suzy had burst into tears and poured her heart out. Sarah had rung Nina at the hotel; she had been so worried about Suzy's outburst. Nina had come home early and brought a bottle of bubbly home. The girls had raised a glass and drunk to Billy and putting the past behind them. They did not mention Billy's name anymore.

Ellie opened the door with a flourish, and a delighted Ellie May threw herself into Sarah's arms. Suzy was beside her, laughing at her daughter's ecstatic greeting. "Ra Ra!" Ellie May said excitedly, in her deep little voice, "Ra Ra here!" Suzy grinned at her friend. "Yes Ell, I know Sarah's here. Let the poor woman get in the door!"

"Hello, my darling!" Sarah said fondly, bending down and kissing Ellie Mays cheek. "Come on inside. I've got something very important to ask you"

"Well, it's about bloody time!" Suzy said to Sarah. She was thrilled for her friend, as Sarah had just told her that she and Jonny were getting married and they wanted Suzy, Nina and Ellie May to be their bridesmaids. Sarah proudly showed off the emerald and diamond engagement ring that Jonny had given to her. She said excitedly that they had gone and chosen it together from a jeweller in Hatton Garden. Jonny had never told Sarah that he had always intended to give her his mother's engagement ring. It had been in his bedside cabinet on the night of the robbery. Billy had stolen it and Jonny and Victor had never seen it again. Billy had sold it to a second hand jeweller on the Isle of Wight. He had lost the money he made from the sale of the ring and various other trinkets he had found in the flat, in the betting shop the very next day.

Ellie May was so excited she was bouncing up and down on the sofa, clapping her hands and saying over and over "Bides maid! Me bides maid!"

Nina was working a late shift at the hotel, so Suzy and Sarah sat and shared tea and biscuits while Ellie May played weddings on the carpet. She had finally stopped jumping up and down. Suzy had given her an old net curtain to play with, and she was parading round the room with it. Sarah had helped Ellie May to fasten the curtain on her head as a veil. She was wearing Sarah's high heel shoes that she had quietly removed from Sarah's feet. She was being a bride and was going to marry "Onny". Ellie May loved Jonny almost as much as she loved

Sarah. The three of them laughed and played together and got married to Jonny until it was time for dinner.

When Ellie May had finally settled down in bed much later, Sarah opened her handbag and determinedly handed Suzy an envelope. "Ooh, what's this, an official invite to the wedding?" Suzy said gleefully, almost snatching the envelope from her friend's outstretched hand. Sarah watched her friend rip open the gold envelope, and said quietly "No Suze. It's not an invitation. It's a present. For you and Ellie. Now, before you start, I'm not taking it back…. My mum gave me a large lump sum after my dad died. It was his life insurance. I want you to share it. I've planned this for a long time, but I had to wait my moment. Now is that time… I know it's not been easy for you, and then there was the news about Billy…anyway, You're my best mate, and I love you and Ellie May to bits. I can't think of a better way to spend it. Blimey, I'm getting all emotional now….I'll shut up.." Suzy gasped as she realised what her friend had given her. She couldn't say a word as she appeared to have a golf ball wedged suddenly in her throat. She seized Sarah in an almighty bear hug and nearly knocked all the stuffing out of her.

Inside the envelope was a cheque for two thousand pounds.

Suzy decided to use some of the money to take Ellie May on her first holiday. Ellie May had had her third birthday and Suzy wanted to give her something special. Nina suggested the Isle of Wight, as she had a lot of contacts on the Island, and told Suzy all the best places to go that she thought Ellie May would enjoy. So Suzy packed her bags, booked the hotel and went for two weeks. Her mum and dad went with her. Suzy insisted on paying for them, and said it was the least she could do after all they had done for her.

Ellie May kept everyone entertained on the ferry going over. Her favourite song was "You are my sunshine" and she sang it sitting on Suzy's lap, over and over, at the top of her voice. Her speech therapy had really begun to pay off. Her voice when she spoke was deep and at times difficult for people to understand, but she loved to sing. "You are my sunshine, my own eeee sunshine.....ooo make me app eeee when skies are gay...." She sang loudly.

"Yes sweet heart" said Suzy, cuddling her little girl on her lap. "You certainly do make me happy when skies are grey. You sing very well, darling. Look up at the sky, Ellie"

Ellie May looked out of the window and up at the sky obediently. It was a little overcast now. Ellie pointed at the clouds with her chubby little finger. "Sky!" she shouted happily. Suzy nodded, and kissed her little daughters head. "Whenever the sun shines through the clouds darling, you remember that that is mummy's love shining down on you. When you feel the warmth of the sunlight on your shoulders, Ellie, that is our love keeping us all nice and warm! My love for you and your love for me! Don't you forget that, darling. Every shaft of sunlight is our love for each other shining down from the sky."

Suzy didn't think Ellie was really listening as she was too excited about her holiday, and Suzy wasn't sure how much of her words she understood. Ellie May was happily breathing on the glass window and drawing squiggles on the glass with her hand, but just as the ferry pulled into the harbour, the sun broke through the clouds. A dazzling shard of gold streamed through the window and Ellie May gave her mum a beaming smile, pulled on Suzy's arm and shouted, "Mum! Look! Love in a sky!"

It had been a beautiful wedding. Carrie had been so proud of her daughter. Sarah had asked her mother to give her away. It was unusual, but Carrie had happily agreed. Proudly they had walked arm in arm down the aisle towards a beaming Jonny. He could not take his eyes off Sarah, and still could not believe his luck. He managed to tear his eyes away for a second to look at his father, and a teary-eyed Marlayna standing beside Victor. Jonny managed a smile at his dad, and Victor winked and gave a nod to his beloved son.

Suzy and Nina had both been bridesmaids along with little Ellie May. They all carried posies of peach coloured roses and they all had peach coloured dresses with cream sashes. Truffle had been allowed to attend the church service, and had a cream bow around his collar. He had slept through the service and Jonny and Sarah had tried their best not to laugh as he snored his way through Jerusalem before they took their vows.

Ellie May had behaved impeccably. She looked good enough to eat in her peaches and cream bridesmaids dress. She stole the show after the service when her headdress fell over her eyes during the photographs, and she pulled it off her head giggling and threw it viciously into the hydrangea bush outside the church, then fell backwards into the bushes. Truffle had dashed towards her, and Ellie May and Truffle had both emerged from the bushes covered in leaves. Truffle had the headdress between his teeth and everyone was in hysterics. It made for some unusual but stunning wedding photographs.

As Sarah and Jonny posed for photographs outside the church, they did not notice the lone figure across the road. It was Louise Blakely Green. She had made it her business to find out about the wedding. She stood in the shadow of the large plane tree and watched as Jonny kissed his bride. Her own huge diamond solitaire engagement ring sparkled on her finger. In a few months' time, she would be a bride herself. Rupert Bingley-Warrington was quite a catch. Her parents were delighted. Rupert was a barrister, as was his father and the family owned a large chunk of Shropshire.

Louise knew her own father was relieved and thought it far enough away from Jonny. He had grown weary and very embarrassed of his daughter's obsession. Rupert's father had found them a great mausoleum of a house, and the happy couple would be moving in after their honeymoon in the Maldives. Now, they had decorators in. Rupert was terribly enthusiastic. He had even hired an interior designer and commissioned special pieces of furniture.

Yes, Rupert really was quite a catch, but he was not Jonny, Louise thought sadly. All her friends had been green with envy when Rupert had popped the question. Especially Camilla, who had hastily married her first serious boyfriend and dropped out of university. She was already on her way to the divorce courts. Louise had told all her friends she was ecstatically happy and they had been pleased for her and not noticed that inside she was screaming. Louise heard the laughter and chatter from the churchyard, and saw the confetti raining down as the photographer snapped away. A single tear coursed down her face and Louise let it dry on her rouged cheek. "Goodbye Jonny" she said quietly. She turned away from the happy scene across the road and briskly walked away.

"So then, Mrs Mason, how's married life treating you?" Jonny smiled mischievously as he held Sarah in his arms. They had been married for a whole ten hours. The reception had just ended and they were alone in the hotel room at last. Sarah looked up at her delicious new husband and smiled radiantly up at him before she replied, "Oh...I think I might get to quite like it"

CHAPTER NINE

1982

Ellie May had settled down very well at school. Suzy had wept buckets on her first day as she waved her daughter off on the bus that came promptly to collect her. She had thought long and hard about the decision to send her to a special needs school rather than a mainstream primary school. Many schools now had a policy of inclusive education, which at first Suzy had been very keen on. She did not want her little girl being singled out as different even though she had Downs.

She had gone to a couple of open days at the local primary schools to see what they had to offer. She had been bitterly disillusioned with both. As far as she could work out, both schools were woefully ill equipped to cope with children like Ellie, and the children with special needs were palmed off with teaching assistants or learning support staff who were poorly trained and didn't have the resources to help the children in their care. Neither of the schools had anything to help Ellie learn, and Suzy worried that she would not get anything out of the education system.

She spoke to a mum who had a ten-year-old Down syndrome boy, and was appalled when she told Suzy that he spent his days playing with building bricks and Lego outside in the corridor with his teaching assistant. His mother had not seen this as unreasonable and was content so long as her son was happy.

Suzy wanted so much more for Ellie May, and was determined to get it. When Suzy went to visit Bonny Ridge School however, Ellie May's face lit up. Bonny Ridge was a school that specialised in caring for special needs children. They had facilities and fully trained staff who understood the individual needs of its pupils and they had amazing specialised equipment. No child in Bonny Ridge ever spent their days excluded from their classmates using building bricks in a corridor. They had lessons that inspired them, and learned practical life skills that would equip them for life in the big bad world. Ellie had spent an ecstatic morning playing in the sensory room, and loved all the lights and soft play areas. Suzy's mind was made up.

The head teacher, Margaret Saunders, introduced Suzy to Ellie Mays Class teacher. Suzy tried to remain calm as she shook Jay Oakland's hand. He was the most divine man Suzy had seen in many a long year. Oh my giddy aunt, she told herself happily. She could not wait to ring Sarah and tell her she thought she was in love.

Suzy was thrilled when Ellie was formally offered a place at Bonny Ridge and started in September. She hoped that Ellie would have the education she deserved, and would do all she was capable of and she hoped with all her heart that Mr Oakland was single and available.

 Suzy tearfully waved her daughter goodbye on her first morning, and told Ellie May that she had filled her daughters pocket with love. "Remember darling, look up at the sky. Don't forget our sunshine. When it shines on you, it means I am thinking of you and you will feel the warmth of mummy's love." Ellie May chuckled, and beamed at her mother. Suzy felt her heart lurch painfully. Life had not always been easy looking after

Ellie May, but Suzy loved her daughter with all her heart. Her innocence, her innate ability to always remain cheerful. A beaming smile was never far away from her dear little face. Suzy forced a smile on to her own face and let go of her little girls hand reluctantly as she stepped on to the school bus.

"OO are my sunshine, my owneee sunshine.." she sang as she climbed up the steps. The escort staff smiled. "Your little ray of sunshine is going to be fine!" said Molly, the driver. "Come on sunshine, wave bye bye to mummy."

It was a beautiful warm sunny Saturday afternoon at the end of September. The nights were beginning to draw in, but the days were still clinging on to the tail end of summer. Sarah and Suzy had taken Ellie May to the park. Nina was working, but would be home by dinnertime.

The girls were looking forward to spending a pleasant evening gossiping over a nice bottle of wine and a Chinese takeaway. Sarah was thrilled to be visiting Suzy for the weekend. Jonny had gone away for the weekend with his dad and Marlayna to an antique's fair. Sarah could have joined them, but thought it would be an ideal opportunity to catch up with her best friend and have a bit of a girly time. Since the wedding, she and Jonny had moved into Jonny's flat and she hadn't spent as much time with Suzy and Ellie May as she would have liked. Sarah had brought face packs for all of them, including Ellie May, nail varnish and manicure sets and all sorts of lotions and potions to keep them happy.Ellie May loved to dress up and look pretty, and she loved it when her Ra Ra painted her nails with "Val narnish".

Suzy was excited, because now Ellie May was happily settled at school, she was going to return to work. Her mum had said she would be more than happy to help out during the school holidays, and Suzy had got in touch with Miss Parish. She had an interview on Monday for her old job. She also told Sarah about her latest meeting with the wonderful Jay Oakland. Suzy had been flirting with him outrageously since Ellie had first started school. She had realised with a jolt that she hadn't had a single boyfriend since Billy. She had not realised it had been so long. Maybe it was time to get back into the swing of things she told herself mischievously, before she signed herself up to a ruddy nunnery. All this celibacy was not doing her any good. She knew it was frowned upon for teachers and parents of pupils at the school to be romantically involved, but she was sure that there was a spark there, and she told Sarah gleefully that she lived in hope.

The two of them chatted excitedly about the arrangements for the interview and Suzy's plans to lure Mr Oakland into a romantic liaison. Sarah told Suzy that the pan stick people were awaiting her return with bated breath, while Suzy pushed Ellie on the swing.

Sarah listened to her friend's excited chatter. She was excited for her. Miss Parish had been such a star, she was sure that the interview was just a formality. Sarah still worked in the gift-wrapping department. She got on very well with Suzy's replacement, Jody, but it wasn't the same without Suzy. Jody was a lovely person, but she didn't have the same sense of humour as Suzy, and the days had been dull without a laugh or two to break the monotony. Now Jody was leaving because her husband had a new job in Dubai. It was the perfect time for Suzy to make her return to the world of ribbons and bows. Sarah could hardly wait. It would be just like old times. She had missed them.

205

Ellie May heard the chimes of the ice cream van as she played happily in the sand pit. "Ice keem?" she said hopefully, standing up abruptly and spilling sand all over the edge of the sand pit. She was looking over at her mum expectantly. Suzy smiled indulgently. "Come on then, artful miss. I don't suppose one little cornet will spoil your dinner. We'll all have one. Bags I a Ninety Nine!"

Ellie May pulled her mother's hand urgently towards the ice cream van. Mummy was taking far too long. Ellie May wanted her to stop talking to Ra Ra and get a move on. Impatiently, she let go of Suzy's hand and bolted toward the open gate of the park. Instinctively, Suzy had reached out and tried to grab her daughter, with Sarah hot on her heels, but Ellie could move incredibly fast when she wanted to, and today she was as slippery as an eel.

Ellie May was so looking forward to her ice cream that she didn't listen to her mummy's frantic calls. She could hear mummy and Ra Ra calling her, and knew they were running after her. She could run very fast now. She pumped her chubby little legs as fast as she could, knowing that Mummy and Ra Ra could never catch her. "Ice keem! Ice keem!" she yelled in delight. She ran towards the nice bright colours of the ice cream van. There was a queue already by the van, and Ellie May was running so fast that she shot past the waiting people and stepped off the curb into the road.

The car was going too fast, and could not stop in time. The driver had been impatient to get home and had thought he could reach the traffic lights before they changed to red. He had not taken much notice of the ice cream van outside of the park. It had been a long hard day. He had been peeved at having to go into the office on a Saturday and he was looking forward to an Indian takeaway with his wife.

Ellie May was flung high into the air amidst the screams of horror from the waiting queue and screech of brakes. She was dead even before she hit the brutally hard tarmac.

CHAPTER TEN

Suzy had not wanted anyone to come back to the flat after the funeral. The service had been so harrowing for her and she had sat in the crematorium beside her mother and father and ashen faced brother in grim silence. Her mother had wept quietly when "You are my sunshine" was played, and Robert, Suzy's brother had held her and let her weep on his shoulder. Suzy had acknowledged all her friends, and was grateful for their support, but she was barely functioning, and could not reach out to them, not today. She saw Sarah's mum, Carrie holding her own mum Joycie and comforting her as the mourners looked at the flowers after the service, but Suzy went to wait in the hearse. She just wanted the day to be over.

Some relatives had gone to the Shakespeare's Head, the pub in Percival Street across the road from the flats, and Sarah, Jonny and Nina had gone to look after them all. Jay Oakland had come along to represent Bonny Ridge School. The school were holding a memorial service for Ellie May when Suzy felt up to it. Suzy had thanked Jay for attending the service but had let Sarah deal with him and all the other mourners. Sarah had been disgusted that Billy's mother Violet had blamed Suzy for the terrible tragedy and had not attended the funeral. Violet had become hysterical upon hearing the terrible news, and had screamed at poor Suzy and accused her of neglect, saying that she couldn't have been looking after her properly. "It's all your fault! How could you be so careless?" she had spat at a stunned Suzy, "Now I've lost everything! First Billy and now Ellie! I wish my son had never bloody met you!"

Carrie had been glad to keep busy, and had made mountains of her now legendary sausage rolls for the buffet. Sarah had wanted so badly to be with Suzy to try to help, but of course, nothing could ease her pain, and Sarah had felt helpless. She had had Jonny to help her and hold her when she cried, but her heart ached at the thought of Suzy having no one to hold her as she sobbed in the night.

Nina had tried to comfort her friend too but Suzy had said she wanted to be left alone. She had hardly said a word since the horrific accident had happened. Suzy remembered sitting in the road and holding the lifeless body of her precious baby in her arms, waiting for the ambulance to arrive. She had cradled her daughter and wished that the terrible howling would stop. She wanted whoever was making the horrible wailing sound to go away and leave her to rock her baby. It wasn't until the ambulance man sat beside her and gently took her arm that she realised that it had been her making the horrible noise.

Everyone had been incredibly kind to her, apart from Violet. Even Narky old Norris from next door had sent flowers, but Suzy was too numb to care. Nothing made sense anymore, and all Suzy wanted to do was go to sleep and never wake up. She was so tired. Every time she closed her eyes, all she could see was her baby, covered in blood and lifeless in her arms. Long into the night she lay, wide eyed, trying to get that vision and the terrible guilt she felt out of her mind. Miss Parish had even rung her to offer her condolences. She had forgotten all about the interview. Sarah must have told her. She couldn't think about that now. She couldn't think about anything. The doctor had given her sedatives, but it was so horrible when she woke up and came back to reality, that she was reluctant to take them.

She stepped out of the big black hearse and fumbled in her bag for her door keys.

Her mum and dad helped her inside and Joycie made tea. She handed her daughter a cup. Suzy took it automatically, and put it down on the coffee table beside her armchair and left it to go cold. Joycie could not bear to see her beautiful daughter look so broken, and her heart ached. She looked at her husband Bob in despair. He had the same look of devastation on his face and Joycie felt helpless. Robert, Suzy's brother came over and gave his mother's shoulder a squeeze. Joycie reached up her arm and held on tight to her son's hand. For a few moments they stayed, all four of them frozen, each lost in their own unbearable grief.

Robert finally broke the silence when he sat down next to Suzy, and let out a little yelp. He had sat on something. He looked under the cushion and pulled out one of Ellie Mays picture books. The hard corner of the book had dug into Robert's leg. Suzy looked over at her brother as he tried to hastily put the book out of sight. "It's alright Rob" Suzy said quietly. "It's all right. That is.. was... Ellie's favourite." Suzy leant across and picked up the book. She smiled sadly and held the book to her chest. Then her face crumpled and she sobbed out all the pain and hurt she felt inside.

Her family gathered round her protectively to share it.

One Year Later.

Sarah had tied a piece of sparkly red ribbon in her hair and had put two bows strategically on her bosom. She poked Suzy who was busy covering a shirt box and said, "How do I look?" Suzy giggled and said with heavy sarcasm "Oh, Jonny is such a lucky, lucky man!"

Eleanor Parish had spotted the two girls from across the shop floor and could not help smiling to herself. It was so good to see Suzy smile. The poor little thing had had more heartache in her young life than any one should have to go through. Life really wasn't fair sometimes. She didn't mind admitting to herself that she had turned a blind eye to the high jinks that they got up to since Suzy had returned to work. Secretly, she rather enjoyed their antics. It was such a refreshing change from the stuffy shirt and tie brigade she usually had to deal with in the office. Most of the older sales assistants on the shop floor were no better, either. She took her job seriously and always tried to remain professional, but there was nothing wrong in having a sense of humour. She often loitered just out of sight just so she could catch a glimpse of the two girls, and would laugh to herself, especially when they took the mickey out of the horrible make up caked women on the cosmetic counters. Eleanor wondered idly to herself where they got the sales staff from who worked in the cosmetics department. They all seemed to come off the same humourless spiteful conveyor belt. They all wore so much make up they would probably crack their faces like china dolls if they tried to smile. It was so refreshing to see the natural beauty of Sarah and Suzy. She really admired young Suzy. The pain in her eyes was still raw and plain to see for anyone sensitive enough to see it, but she had a quiet dignity about her. She had managed to get her life back after her terrible tragedy. Now, that took guts. She loved to go home at the end of the day and tell Catherine all about the antics that the gift-wrap girls got up to.

Eleanor ducked out of sight as the hideous woman from the Clarins counter tried to catch her eye. She was bound to be about to complain about something trivial as usual, and Eleanor had more important things to deal with. The handsome customer had asked her for directions, and she was very happy to direct him once she realised who he was looking for.

"Quick, Miss Parish is coming!" Suzy hissed to Sarah. Suzy ducked below the counter to compose herself while Sarah hastily removed her bosom bows, and yanked the sparkly ribbon out of her hair. She dropped it on the floor behind the counter. Miss Parish had a tall dark haired man behind her and she smiled and said, "Here you are, sir. This is our gift wrapping counter" she winked at Sarah and walked swiftly away.

Suzy popped her head up from behind the counter and her eyes opened wide in surprise. Standing in front of her was Ellie Mays teacher Jay Oakland.

Suzy was nervous about her lunch date. Fancy Jay Oakland asking her out! She suddenly realised she still had not been on a date since Billy, and the least said about that the better. She was woefully out of practise. She had not seen Jay since Ellie

May's school memorial service two months ago. The school had waited until Suzy felt up to it. It had been an incredibly emotional day of course, and they had only spoken a few pleasantries at the time. Suzy had mentioned that she would be going back to work though. She could not believe that Jay had taken the trouble to seek her out. She felt a bit guilty, and asked Sarah if she thought it would look bad if she went. Sarah said indignantly "Oh Suze, of course you should go! Why should you feel guilty?" she saw her friend's eyes fill with tears, and she hugged her. They were still behind the counter at the time, and Sarah was sure the pan stick people were eavesdropping, but she didn't care. She let Suzy go and said gently, "Suze, you mustn't feel guilty. No one could have loved that little girl more than you did. What happened was a terrible thing, and I know you'll never get over it. How could you? But it doesn't mean you can't ever be happy. Ellie May was always happy, wasn't she?" Suzy gave a tearful nod. "Well then, she would want you to be happy too, wouldn't she? She hated it if one of us was upset. Now go on, you go and have a nice time, and if he asks you out again, you better ruddy well say yes, lady, or I will staple your arse to the bow making machine"

Suzy realised after her second vodka and tonic that she was actually having a really good time. It was a pity she had to go back to work, and she knew she couldn't risk having another drink, or else she probably wouldn't go back after lunch. The time was whizzing by. Jay Oakland was witty, intelligent and incredibly sexy. He smelled divine and his eyes were the twinkliest blue she had ever seen. This was the first date she had been on in years, and it felt good. For the first time since Ellie had died, Suzy did not feel weighed down by her sorrow. Her heartache was still there, of course, and she knew it would never truly leave her. Nor did she want it to, but Suzy thought that maybe she could allow herself a bit of light relief now.

When she smiled across the table at Jay, her smile did not quite meet her eyes yet, but she was hopeful. Maybe one day soon, she told herself. One day, she would feel able to move on.

 She took another sip of her drink. As she did so the sun came out from behind a cloud, and a shaft of golden sunlight beamed across the table and lit up her face.

EPILOGUE

Five Years Later

Carrie Miller left the women's refuge where she worked as a volunteer and strolled happily along the street. She loved her job, and was so glad that Sarah had persuaded her to apply for it. It had given her a whole new lease of life. She wasn't considering retirement any time soon. She saw so many women on a daily basis with the same broken spirit that she used to have and it was remarkable and heart-warming to see them progress over time. She had blossomed herself and her own personal transformation had been a real surprise to her. She had recently had her hair done too and looked very chic. Sarah regularly took her clothes shopping now, and her wardrobe was smart and stylish. She hardly recognised herself these days. She looked and felt at least ten years younger than she really was. When she looked in the mirror now, she no longer saw the cowed haunted woman she used to be. She still occasionally woke up afraid in the middle of the night, but once her drowsy brain realised that she was safe and warm in her own bed, she soon drifted back off to sleep. The guilt had almost left her. The secret that she still shared with her beloved daughter Sarah was now locked deep inside both of them, and Carrie felt she had finally come to terms with what she had done. They never spoke of it anymore. It was a secret that Carrie knew the pair of them would carry to their graves. Sometimes, Carrie still felt guilty about the burden she had put upon her daughters shoulders. She did not think it was entirely fair that Sarah had to keep such a secret from the husband she adored. Sarah however, would not talk about it, and Carrie had been forced to accept the silence.

Carrie loved Fridays. She finished work at lunchtime on Friday and usually did a bit of shopping before spending the afternoon with Sarah and Lydia, her beautiful little granddaughter. Today she was meeting Sarah and Lydia for lunch, and then they were going home together. She had been looking forward to it all morning. Suzy and her little girl, Amy would be meeting them, along with Suzy's mum, Joycie. All girls together.

They all loved their girly days. They were going for a nice lunch. Suzy had told Sarah that Nina would be coming too. Carrie liked Nina. She missed seeing her around now she had her own little flat, but she tried to visit whenever she had time off work. Jonny and his father and Marlayna had gone away for the weekend to an antiques fair, so Sarah and Lydia were coming to stay for the whole weekend. Carrie could not wait to see Sarah and Lydia's face when Jonny got back. He had confided in Carrie that he was bringing home a black Labrador puppy as a surprise for his girls. They had all been devastated when Truffle had died in his sleep two months ago. He had reached the ripe old age of twelve and although grey around his muzzle had remained sprightly right up until the end. Victor had put his ashes on the mantelpiece in pride of place and had a special plaque made. It had been set into the ground in Truffle's favourite spot in the back garden. Carrie hoped the new little puppy would help them to recover from the loss. He would certainly keep them entertained.

Last night Carrie had made sausage rolls for the girls to have later at home, because Lydia and Amy both loved them, and she would make fairy cakes with the little girls later as they loved to help her bake. She had left their little aprons out all ready for them, and pictured the excited chatter and smell of baking wafting through her little flat. She smiled to herself as she wondered along the busy street. She never took her freedom for granted. She was reminded of her old life every day at work and knew she was incredibly fortunate. Joycie had asked her once over a cup of tea if she ever felt lonely, living on her own and without hesitation, she had said a vehement "No" and shook her head. She was quite content. She had her girls for company, Jonny was always willing to help her out if she needed any DIY doing, but she had become very self-sufficient and hardly ever needed to call upon his services now. She was very grateful that she saw Sarah and Lydia almost every day, and regularly saw Suzy and her beautiful little girl, Amy. Joycie had become a very close friend and Carrie even had a social life. She never felt old. Well, hardly ever, she told herself ruefully. Maybe from time to time in the winter when her arthritis played up.

It gladdened her heart to see Suzy happy and settled after the tragedy she had been through. Jay was a wonderful husband and father. Suzy looked radiant, especially now she was expecting again.

Carrie Spotted Sarah and little Lydia, just ahead on the corner waiting for her. She smiled broadly, raised her arm and waved. Lydia waved back excitedly and ran towards her, arms outstretched to hug her beloved Nana.

Carrie scooped the giggling child up in her arms and smothered her little face in kisses. It was going to be a fantastic weekend.

The End

ACKNOWLEDGEMENTS

Thank you to my son Lewis and my husband Ken for helping me with the tricky technical bits. Thanks also to my husband for his patience and understanding when I lose myself in writing and he becomes a writer's widower.

To my two dogs for always being by my side as I work on my laptop. I am sure the endless supply of dog hair and slobber helps with the flow of words.

To my friends. There are not enough words to thank you enough. Just know you have my unswerving admiration and knowing you are always there to fight my corner fills me with pride and love.

My family mean everything to me. This book is dedicated to the memory of my mother Mary and my father Fred. I still miss them every day.

I am a proud member of famousfiveplus.com an online group for independent authors. I am so grateful for the help and support I receive from all its talented members and in particular to Pauline Barclay the founder of this amazing group.

If you or any one you know is suffering in silence from domestic abuse, please know that there is help out there. Do not put up with it. Please get that help. Contact 1in4women.com for advice.

Printed in Great Britain
by Amazon